THE SAILORS OF SVALGSAY

The Sixth Book of
Dubious Magic

In memory of Paul – still miss you, mate.

And as ever, for my darling bride.

CONTENTS

1 TAKING A SHOT

Retired Colonel Gilbert Hastings liked to believe he still cut a dignified figure as he took his morning walk along the beach. His back was still straight, and his stride still confident. Unlike others he sometimes saw, he walked the dog - she didn't walk him despite her size. She was an Irish wolfhound named Princess Louise after the original patron of Hastings' old regiment, the Argyll and Sutherland Highlanders.

There were no other dog walkers this morning. There seldom were at this hour, and this time of year, but the old soldier was a man of habit. Neither the half-light nor the cold wind off the North Sea deterred him.

The colonel was mildly surprised to see another figure on the beach though – a jogger. 'Dunna get a lot of them along here. Obviously a tourist. Not something you'd see a local doing!' he thought.

As they approached each other Hastings nodded approvingly at the visitor's apparel. Well rugged up against the wind. Thick black jumper and track pants. Gloves – sensible. Woolen hat, or was it a balaclava?

The old man smiled at that thought. Balaclava was where his regiment had first won fame during the Crimean War, when 500 men had faced down a force of over 20,000 Russians. Long before his time, of course, but still a source of pride.

Absorbed in his reverie, Colonel Hastings was scarcely aware of the jogger changing course slightly to run straight at him. He completely failed to notice the gun being pulled from the waistband of the track pants.

He barely felt the bullet as it entered his brain, and was dead before his body hit the sand.

Princess Louise strained at her leash, still held tightly in the colonel's lifeless hand. The jogger hadn't broken stride. Another bullet and the dog collapsed beside her master, a strikingly similar hole just above and between the eyebrows.

There had been no sound. A silencer fitted to the pistol ensured that. Not that there was anyone else on the beach anyway. Just two bodies, a few seabirds, and the shooter in black, trotting steadily but unhurriedly away.

*

The Northlink ferry *M.V. Hjlatland* was on its way into Lerwick. She'd set off from Kirkwall in the Orkneys a little before midnight on her regular off-season Thursday night run. For the next few months she would only sail overnight on Thursdays, Saturdays and Sundays – mostly for the sake of local residents travelling between the islands and the mainland. The weather deterred a lot of people from casual travelling.

Brisk would be an understatement. It was, as the brunette standing beside her boyfriend looking out over the water said, "Bloody cold". They both wore lined weatherproof coats, hers over a warm shirt and jumper, his over a purple t-shirt. They snuggled close together, each with an arm around the other's waist while the other hand gripped the handrail, wary of the boat's pitching.

They'd been awake for a while, and after enjoying some mutual self-indulgence had eventually decided to vacate their very snug cabin for some fresh air. It was a clear night. With luck, the lights of their destination might be visible. If not, well, there was a lot to be said for starlight.

They were out on deck even though it was still dark, taking the pre-dawn air before the breakfast to be laid on early. A 7:30 arrival meant passengers had to be fed at an hour many wouldn't normally consider on a holiday. At this time of year though, few of those on board were holidaying. Even these two were coming to the islands for business as much as pleasure.

Her head on his shoulder, she asked, "Do you think this is really a good idea, babe?"

"Hey, it's *your* idea, pretty lady, and I've never known you to have a dud one."

"Why, thank ya, kind sir!"

"I just calls 'em as ah sees 'em, ma'am."

The phony Southern drawls probably wouldn't have fooled anyone, but they were a little affectation they'd developed over a long period of what had started out as harmless flirting.

"Seriously though babe," she said, "I've never tried anything like this before. Never even thought to try it. It's not like anyone's ever encouraged me – until you that is. Why should I think I'd be any good at it?"

"Equally seriously, sweetheart, it's my belief that you'll be good at absolutely anything you put your mind to. It strikes me that that's always been the case before."

She stared out across the sea. The lights of the ferry caught the whitecaps so they looked to dance with brilliant life.

"Not always. There've been some failures along the way, some more spectacular than others. My marriage to Sonny wasn't exactly a great success."

The arm around her waist moved to around her shoulders. He turned to look into her green eyes. The most beautiful eyes in his world.

"It takes two to make a relationship work. You're not to blame for his failings. If he was in any way disappointed with you then the problem was with his expectations. Probably his perception, too, in my less than humble opinion. And this is different. This is about your ambition – *your* goal. Your abilities and talent. The only disappointment will be if you don't at least try."

"Thank you, babe. I'm going to give it my best shot."

They smiled at each other and kissed, long and loving and supportive.

They were going to need that mutual support.

.o0o.

2 HANGING AROUND

Her cheeks flaming to almost match the colour of her hair, the girl got up from her barstool and stormed out of the *Hangman's Arms*, heedless of the squall out on the street. The man seated beside the place she'd just vacated leered after her, calling, "Och, ye know ye want it, lass!"

He grabbed the glass of wine she'd abandoned and drained it at a gulp. "Waste not, want not," he said as he wiped a dribble of claret from his chin and made to follow her.

"Basher – don't do it, eh?" said the publican pleadingly.

Basher stood, apparently weighing his options as he looked back and forth between the bar and the lass who was retreating into the rain.

"Gie us a drink then, Tam," he finally said and sat back down.

His folded arms made it clear that he didn't expect to pay for the order – a bribe to avoid trouble. He looked around the room to see who else might be worth his attentions. A quiet night. No more single women. No great matter. Basher Gurley treated his own marriage with contempt, and had the same regard for anyone else's relationships. He scanned the *Hangman's Arms* like a predator checking a herd to find the most vulnerable animals.

A couple of locals he knew and didn't fancy. Brunette in a checked shirt with one of those vests with a dozen pockets – nice olive skin, blue eyes – not bad. Bloke with her looked vaguely familiar. Tough, too. At another table, there's another brunette. Pretty. Interesting green eyes – hmm, she might be a fighter. Sitting with her, a scruffy bloke in a purple t-shirt, he'd be no problem, and that tour guide Alan Munro. Munro's an old man. He'd be no problem either, but people knew him and liked him enough that maybe the girl wasn't worth the trouble. Maybe. Depending on other options.

Dark haired girl over by the corner near the door. Pale skin. One of them Goth types. Kinda pretty, even if the silver ring in her nostril made it look like she'd sneezed but not wiped her nose properly. Boyfriend with the same sort of look. An attempt at a beard that looked as though it had been flicked on with an almost-dry paintbrush. Glasses with those black frames like Buddy Holly used to wear. Yeah, she'd do.

Clutching his lager, Basher swaggered to the Goth couple's table and sat down on the bench seat beside the girl, trapping her against the wall.

"You're nae from around here," he stated. "Welcome tae Shetland."

"Um, thanks…" stammered the young man sitting opposite.

"I'm nae talkin' tae you, pal. I think you should go tae the bar, sit and have yerself a wee chat wi' Tam there, while this lassie and I get acquaint-ed."

"Hey, hang on! I…" the young man started to protest.

Gurley leaned over the wooden table. He didn't touch the youth, but loomed close enough to steam the lenses of his glasses. Glaring, he growled, "I'm suggestin' tae ye nicely noo, pal. Ye dinna want me tae be not nice, do ye?"

Basher grabbed the girl's upper arm, drawing a whimper from her. "Now, away wi' ye!" he said.

With a helpless look toward his girlfriend the pale young man slipped from his bench and scurried to the bar. Tam was sympathetic enough to hand him a drink on the house, but made no move to assist.

Watching from her nearby table the green-eyed brunette quietly said to her companions, "I don't believe that creep! How does he get away with it?"

Alan Munro sighed. "He's him a laad o' him, I'm afraid. A bad character," he explained, seeing Elizabeth's blank expression. "John Gurley used tae be… well, he was never a *good* man, he's been called Basher since he was little more than a bairn. But he wasnae the same after the Gulf War, ye ken? He always had a bit o' a mean streak but after he came back fra' Iraq there were a want aboot him - he wasnae quite right in the heid. Tam saw service in the Falklands himself so he cut the lad some slack. For too long, I fear. Noo the bad habits are ingrained. Tae be honest, I think most folks are a bit faird o' Basher. Fearful, ye ken? He's aye well named, especially when he's fit fer tyin'. In a rage, I mean."

"Well, somebody should bloody stand up to him," snapped the woman. "Come on babe, work some of your hex on him!"

The man in the purple t-shirt sighed. "You know it's not that easy, sweetheart. It's not like I can control how the magic works, and I don't really want to wish permanent harm on anyone, even a richly deserving toerag like that one."

Munro looked puzzled by the exchange. At the sound of a yelp from the beleaguered girl all three of them turned toward the table by the door, where Gurley had evidently transferred his grip to the Goth's upper leg.

The shaggy haired man in purple ground his teeth. "But I do take your point, Q," he said. Folding his arms and glaring at Basher Gurley he said, "I wish you'd cool off - let go of the lass and get out of here. Go take a running jump."

"And go to hell!" added the woman he'd called Q.

"That too," he added with a grin for her benefit.

Alan Munro shook his head. He'd been leading this Australian couple around the Shetlands for a few days. It was the very tail end of The Season so they were his only clients. A genial man anyway, Alan had rather taken a shine to the pair. Their love for each other was probably more obvious than they realised, but there were moments when their conversation was… *difficult* to follow.

It wasn't just the Down Under slang or accents. There were moments when they were already sounding a bit like locals in conversation, he'd noticed – not deliberately, more like natural mimics. It was more as if they had their own code. Things mutually understood but not said overtly, or in ways that made no sense to him.

There was a sudden gust of cold damp air as the door of the *Hangman's Arms* swung open. A small crowd of young men staggered in roistering loudly. A Buck's Night or Stag Party was as instantly recognizable in Shetland as it was in Australia. Several of them had the look and dress of the Goth style favoured by Basher's 'target' and her beau. Looking up at precisely the wrong moment Basher got a faceful of sleet.

Gurley jumped to his feet, fists balled, and then stopped. He liked a fight, and under certain circumstances didn't mind a numerical disadvantage. But some of these buggers were his size, or more. And he wasn't carrying hardware like he used to be allowed to.

At the head of the new arrivals was a large fellow with a shaved crown, long flowing beard, and a ponytail that reached down past his shoulder blades.

"Ahoy Steve! There ye are!" he cried, spotting the bespectacled Goth at the bar.

The pale skinned girl seized the opportunity of Basher standing to slip past him and dash to the bar to join Steve. The would-be ravisher snarled. What sort of idiot took his girl with him on a night out with his mates? Not that he'd had any actual mates for a long time.

He stood in a small fury of indecision. Was she worth a fight? Probably not – too skinny really. What about the other options? The green-eyed lass? Nah – even Basher's compromised brain recognised that if looks could kill he'd already be worm meat. The girl in the checked shirt looked bored with the big guy, but aye, he was big. Wearing khaki and camo gear too. Might even *be* an ex-soldier. Probably an officer. Looked arrogant enough. Might be good to take him down a notch, but again, was she worth the trouble?

Then, as he cast his eyes around he noticed a face outside. The figure
was wrapped up in a black hoodie and scarf against the weather, but he'd
caught a glimpse of beautifully sculpted Scandinavian features and a wisp
of blonde hair. He was sure he saw a wink in his direction. That'd do
him.

Not coming into the *Hangman's*? Well, he didn't really blame her. Probably heading for the *Royal Anne*. He knew he wasn't welcome in there,
but didn't care. If he could catch up with her first he could take her somewhere else anyway. He knew a few quiet dark corners in Lerwick.

After quickly downing the last of his beer Basher headed out into the
street with some haste, trying to keep an eye on where the blonde was
going.

As the door swung shut behind him green-eyed Q grinned. "Well done,
JB. Not quite a run but close enough, and he's out of here, which is most
important."

Her given name was Elizabeth McKew – only her purple shirted boyfriend John B. Stewart was permitted to use the affectionate nickname.

Stewart returned the grin and squeezed her hand. "Thanks, pretty lady.
And you know, the further away from here he takes his running jump the
better, as far as I'm concerned. I don't need to see it."

They both laughed. Alan chuckled politely, not quite understanding the
joke.

The couple hadn't explained to their guide that John B. was a wizard. Not
in the conventional sense, if there is such a thing as a conventional wizard.
But ever since his head had collided forcefully with a poker machine in
Canberra (a substantial quantity of single malt whisky had been involved)
Stewart had found that his wishes came true.

Not quite predictably – he was learning to choose his words with care
although that still didn't sit easily with an impulsive nature. He'd also

found himself drawn into conflict with a variety of strange threats – an insane sorceress, dark and ancient gods, a homicidal Hawaiian volcano worshipper, a father and daughter who used dreams to kill, even a mad Russian scientist. It was the demise of the latter that had inadvertently made John B. Stewart a wealthy man. That wasn't public knowledge, either.

The money was discreetly held in a Swiss bank account that only he could access. He quietly used it to sustain a very ordinary credit card that only rarely slipped into debit. He thought of it as his 'magic pudding' – take a piece out and it topped itself back up again. It meant he'd been able to walk away from the Public Service job he'd long ago ceased to enjoy, and take opportunities to travel as they presented themselves.

Out on the rain-slicked street Basher had lost sight of his quarry. Couldn't have been heading for the *Royal Anne* after all. Must have turned into one of the side streets. Down this one? Aye – there was a slim figure in black down near the bottom of the steep hill that led to the waterfront. Must be heading for the *Brigand.* That was a good sign. It was Basher's sort of pub, except that not many women went there. The ones that did were usually pretty available though, or at least negotiable.

He sped up, breaking into a run as the dark figure turned left, out of his line of sight. His foot slipped on the wet sloping path and he performed an awkward uncoordinated hop skip and a jump before landing with a painful splash, head down in the gutter.

Gurley cursed as a small torrent of rainwater streamed into his trouser leg. Struggling to his feet he found that he was stained with gutter slime from armpit to ankle. Even Basher realised that looking like this he had no chance of picking up a bird. For as much as he'd force his attentions on the unwilling, he persisted in the belief that deep down they really wanted him.

Muttering and cursing he strode off for home, kicking viciously at any bottle or can he encountered. Woe betide any cat that might cross his path, black or otherwise. It would be a tough night for his wife. Again.

Back in the *Hangman's Arms* the buck's party that included the Goths was getting loud and boisterous. The tall character who'd led the group in was leaning heavily on one of his companions and pointing to the man in khaki.

"'Ere, Brian, izzat no' that man off the telly? The yin that does all yon dangerous adventures an' eatin' weird stuff like animal poo?"

"Eh? Don't be daft, Fergal. Why'd a mannie like that be in Lerwick?"

"Well it bloody looks like him!"

"Aye, it does right enough – but it cannae be the same guy, I tell ye."

"Och, I s'pose not."

The girl in the checked shirt grinned. It was hard not to hear the supposedly discreet conversation. "I don't think the locals reckon the Shetlands are dangerous enough for you, Miskwa," she said with a laugh.

"Well, I've certainly been in much tougher places than this *Hangman's Arms*, despite the name, Jayne. I remember a bar we found in the back streets of Cape Town after I'd finished the walk across the Ngorongoro Crater…"

Jayne managed to not roll her eyes as Miskwa Burns launched into another of his interminable stories. She was his cinematographer, stuck with filming his latest supposedly one-man expedition. Perhaps that was why the television adventurer had chosen her as his film crew – so he could truthfully call it a one *man* effort.

As challenging as the forthcoming sail journey over to Scandinavia and up across the Arctic Circle would be, she really didn't envy the job of the poor editor who would have to try to make Burns' egocentric ramblings into exciting television.

The Australians and their tour guide watched the events around them from their table.

"I'm sorry, folks. The *Hangman* isnae the best o' wir bars, I'm afraid. I should ha' taken ye over tae the *Royal Anne*," said Munro apologetically.

"Not to worry, Alan. There'll be plenty of time to get there," said John B. "We've plenty yet to see and do around the islands, and Lerwick's the ideal base."

 Elizabeth smiled. "The last few days getting the feel of the place has been lovely – I'm so glad it's late in the season and we've got you all to ourselves! Now I want to really start to get into the history!"

'Both the Shetlands' and my own,' was what she didn't say out loud.

.o0o.

3 WHOS, WHYS AND WHEREFORES

John B. and Elizabeth's journey to the Shetlands had been not quite a spur of the moment decision. They'd left their erstwhile travelling companions Wilko and Jazz (Robert Wilkes and Jacinta Parrish were the names on their passports) on the southern Hebridean island of Islay. Jazz was finishing up her contract as a consultant engineer at a small distillery in the village of Sron Dubh. That was where they'd encountered the murderous dream weavers. The wizard and his ladylove had flown to Glasgow and spent several days exploring the city's charms.

John B. was more than happy to bankroll their travels courtesy of the Swiss account, but Q was not long divorced from a control freak. While she had full confidence that Stewart was a very different man she was determined to make a significant contribution of her own.

Her divorce settlement had given her enough financial security to walk away from the same Canberra office that Stewart had left – they'd been workmates and friends for a few years before discovering that they'd fallen in love.

Now she was feeling the bite of the travel bug, but she'd wondered how best to fund it. Inspiration had struck one night over drinks in a bar that had formerly been a church. The lights had been designed to illuminate the beautiful stained glass windows that still dominated the space. Particularly catching Q's eye was a panel that featured an open Bible. It wasn't the scripture that struck her so much as the image of the book. That was it! She would write!

While on Islay she'd gone to a lecture presented by the local historical society and been inspired by what she heard. She knew a little of her own family history, but only a little. Enough to know that there was a Viking connection via the islands to the north of Scotland. Her mother Myra had pointedly not often discussed the man who fathered Elizabeth. Berated him a lot, but not discussed him. 'Write about what you know,' was a good maxim, she realised. The more she got to know of the Norse/Scottish connection the more she felt the tug of a story there.

John B. knew that once Q was determined to do something, the thing would be done. That determination had saved his life in the not too distant past. If she wanted to be an author, then that book was going to happen.

He wanted to help, and not just to make her happy. Sure, her face lit up when she talked about 'the saga' as bits of it occurred to her, but he quickly realised as she talked that there *was* a good story in her head. He wanted to hear it. Read it.

"How much do you know about your Dad?" he'd asked.

"Not a lot. He skipped out on my mother just after I was born. She only ever referred to him as 'The Mistake' after that, although she was old-fashioned enough to keep his name and pass it on to me. She was scathing about anything Scottish, which is how I knew this was where he came from."

"Any idea of where, exactly? It may not look it on a globe, but once you get here – well, it's a big place, sweetheart."

Elizabeth smiled. "I think I've got a clue. When I was about fourteen I remember we were watching a TV documentary about 'civilian heroes of World War Two'. There was a piece about some fishing boats that smuggled escaped POWs from Europe - Scandinavia, over to the Shetland Islands. 'Not that wretched place!' she said and almost tore the channel changer off the TV set. I asked her about it. She said, 'Your father came from some place with a ridiculous name… Board something… yes, Boardastubble, somewhere up there'. She never mentioned it again but the name stuck in my head because I liked the sound of it."

A certain amount of library, internet and newspaper research later, the couple had found that yes, there was a little place with that unlikely name, best known for a nearby 'standing stone' of ancient origin. They'd also found an advertisement for the services of *"Alan Munro: Tour Guide –*

No-one knows the Shetlands like a local!" and booked themselves onto the ferry *M.V. Hjlatland.*

The drive from Glasgow up to Aberdeen was beautiful, but with Elizabeth 'on a mission' they didn't linger to enjoy the scenery as much as they otherwise might have. That would happen on the return journey, they promised themselves. Likewise when the ferry called in at the Orcadian capital Kirkwall. The rich history of the Orkneys would doubtless provide grist for Q's creative mill, but she was determined that the islands to the north were to be where she'd start.

Alan had met them at the dock and helped them to find the *Ernster Guesthouse* where they'd booked a comfortable room, decorated with genuine old-fashioned charm, including a four-poster bed and pillows stuffed with feathers from local geese (or so they were assured). The walls of the guesthouse were adorned with images of the sea eagles that gave the place its name, which translated as 'Eagle Farm'.

Having only had Elizabeth's objective explained to him in broad terms – she didn't yet have precise details in her own head – Alan then spent three days driving them around the 'mainland' and the island of Yell to its north as an 'orientation' to the Shetlands.

The place was a treasure trove of history. Over five thousand years of habitation were reflected in boundary dykes, cairns, burial chambers, ruined chapels and farmhouses. All these structures were made of stone, timber having always been a rare and precious resource on the islands.

There were pieces of Pictish prehistory, vestiges of Viking villages, and crumbling chunks of early Christian chapels. Some sites showed clear evidence of waves of occupation, with medieval walls rising from prehistoric foundations sitting alongside the remains of Iron Age fortifications.

Alan Munro's pride in his home was evident, and his two clients appreciated and quickly shared his enthusiasm. Elizabeth was starting to build a mental catalogue of elements she could use in her planned book. She was also becoming increasingly interested in the prospect of having a family connection to the Shetlands.

The morning after the fleeting encounter with Basher Gurley dawned bright and clear, if chilly. The rain had blown back out to sea leaving the air smelling crisp. But when Alan arrived at the guesthouse the Australians quickly noticed that he wasn't his usual cheery self.

"Is everything okay, mate? You seem a bit… not quite with it this morning," said John B.

"Och, sorry folks," said the guide. "Had some disturbin' news this mornin'. A local feller's been killed."

"Oh, I'm sorry," said Elizabeth. "A friend of yours?"

"No' exactly. The Colonel kept himsel' tae himsel' for the most part. We'd talk politely enough if we met, mind. Nasty business," said Munro, more to himself than his clients.

"A bad accident you mean?" asked the brunette, envisaging something like a fall off one of the Shetland's dramatic cliffs.

Munro looked uncomfortable. "No miss. A murder."

The couple exchanged glances. Since hitting his head that time in Canberra John B. had developed an unfortunate knack of finding himself in weird and dangerous situations. It wasn't the first murder he'd been in close proximity to.

"Was there anything… unusual about it, do you know?" asked the wizard cautiously.

Munro gave him a puzzled, rather affronted look. "I'd ha' thought that any murder wasnae a usual thing. They're certainly no' common around here."

"No, of course. Sorry, I… ah…"

"Sorry Alan, there's a book of supernatural stories in the lounge of the guesthouse. John B. was reading it over breakfast and I think it's fired his imagination," explained Elizabeth, deftly defusing any awkwardness.

"Ach, aye. I understand. There's a lot o' the uncanny aboot the islands, right enough. But this wasnae like that. A mystery, aye, but nothing supernatural aboot it. Somebody shot Colonel Hastings down on Meal Beach, over on West Burra a few days ago apparently. Shot his poor old *hund*, too – his dog. Both o' them, right through the *harnpan*. The brain-box. Police are asking for witnesses – anyone around the beach in the early hours o' Friday mornin'. Nobody's come forward, though."

"Friday morning. That's when we arrived," John B. observed quietly. It sounded a bit like paranoia, but his life in recent months might excuse that. And just because you're paranoid it doesn't mean you're wrong.

Oblivious to his shaggy client's musings Alan shrugged. "Ach aye, but this happened well before the ferry came in accordin' tae my pal Jimmy. He's one o' the local policemen. He called round tae my place this mornin'. Told me aboot it and asked me tae keep ma eyes and ears open while we're travellin' aboot. I get around the islands a lot more than most folk."

Alan's mood seemed to have been lifted by the act of sharing the story, as is often the case. 'A burden shared is a burden halved' may be a cliché, but it got to be one by frequently being true.

"West Burra – that's south of Scalloway, isn't it? We went there to look at that Pictish stone in the graveyard, didn't we?"

"Aye, Miss Elizabeth. We actually went past the beach turn-off on wer way doon tae Papil, where the stone stands," said Munro, a little ruefully although there was no way he could have known of the Colonel's fate at the time.

The guide squared his shoulders and continued. "I thought today I'd gie ye a choice. There's a bonny museum just doon the way at Hay's Dock. Ye might like tae spend the day there. A lot o' verra good stuff frae right across the history o' the Shetlands, frae their first formin', pre-history, Iron Age – right up tae World War Two and the most recent stuff, alternative power an' the like. The other thought was tae drive up and get the ferry over tae Unst. There's a fine wee Heritage Centre up at Haroldswick. It'd also gie us the chance tae go tae Boardastubble since ye said ye had an interest there, Miss Elizabeth."

John B. gazed out at the clearing sky. "I vote we leave the local museum for a day when the weather's not so fair for driving. What do you think, my love? Do you fancy a day on Unst – you could get stuck into your family history?"

Elizabeth nodded as she reached across the table to squeeze Stewart's hand. "Thanks babe." She turned to the guide and said, "Thank you, too Alan. Can we start with Boardastubble before we go to the Heritage Centre, please? I think I've waited long enough to find out something about my father."

During the pleasant drive north to the little vehicular ferry Elizabeth explained to Alan the little she knew of the paternal side of her family. It was a story she'd told very few people, and none to the detail she'd shared with John B.

From the ferry landing they headed northwest along a narrow, mostly sealed road that took them past a series of small fields. Several had broken down vehicles placed prominently in their midst. Alan explained that these had proved much more effective than the old scarecrows at deterring the flocks of migratory geese that periodically wreaked havoc on the crops.

"I thought a couple of the trucks and cars looked remarkably well maintained, besides the absence of wheels," said Stewart.

"Aye well, geese arenae daft – they've an idea what a wreck looks like, and that it cannae hurt them," Munro grinned as he explained.

Their first brief stop before the little village was to look at the solitary standing stone that gave the place its name.

"Said tae be from the Old Norse for 'battle-axe pillar' according tae the scholars," the guide explained.

John B. nodded distractedly as he stared at the stone. "*Börðu-stöpull*, that sounds about right – you can see it in the shape," the wizard agreed.

Munro stared in turn at his customer, who'd shown no previous indication of speaking the antique Scandinavian tongue. Elizabeth smiled and patted Alan's arm sympathetically. She'd had a little experience of her beau's propensity for knowing little bits of unexpected languages, and had heard more from Wilko. Stewart always dismissed it as 'having read quite a bit, and it seems to just come to mind when I need it.' Not a very satisfactory explanation, she thought, but none better was forthcoming.

"So, like much of the north, it's an old Viking settlement? I wonder if the McKews are part of that heritage…" the brunette mused.

As he led the pair back to his vehicle Alan said, "Tae be truthful, Miss Elizabeth, it's no a name I can recall hearin' around these parts. But I do have an idea o' where tae look. Best place to start is to pay a call on an old pal o' mine. Was a policeman around these parts for years and knew most everyone."

Retired sergeant Rory McGregor and his wife lived in a well restored old croft on the edge of the village. The stone walls inside had been plastered and painted in a soft yellow. The home wasn't large, but it was comfortable and welcoming.

When his visitors arrived, McGregor was engrossed in reconstructing one of the old dry stone walls edging the neighbouring field. It was meticulous work, for which the former policeman's patient methodical nature was ideally suited. On being introduced, he insisted they all come inside for a pot of tea.

As McGregor washed his hands in a tub of rainwater just outside the back door of the croft, Munro recounted what he knew of the murder of Colonel Hastings.

"Tha's a bad business, right enough Alan. Och, ye'd nae like tae think it was a local – Hastings was a bit of a crotchety old bugger, but if that were a killin' offence there'd be damn few folk left on the islands!"

"Whit's all this talk o' killing?" asked Rory's wife Mary, who'd heard the last of that comment as the foursome entered the croft.

At a nod from Rory, Alan again recounted the story. Mary's brow creased in concern as she pulled a tray of scones from the oven.

"It'll be some o' them young louts in Scalloway," she said with some force. "They come in on their boats noo wi' too much money, and too much drink in them, and old Hastings didnae take kindly tae their carryin' on."

McGregor looked thoughtful. "Aye, he'd speak his mind right enough – as many folk around here do," he said with a look towards his wife who, fortunately for him was concentrating on setting her scones on a rack at the time. "He might have gotten intae a *kallishang* – whit would ye call it, an angry argument - upset somebody off one o' the fishing boats."

"It'd be a very unusual sort of somebody if that was the case," remarked John B. When the others looked at him in surprise and puzzlement he continued. "As you've described it, Alan, it doesn't sound like his murder was a spur of the moment thing, like you'd get if the old bloke had angered someone that had too many drinks in him – someone like that charmer we saw in the *Hangman's Arms*. Shot from close range, no sign of a struggle, and the killing of the dog – it all sounds, well, clinical. Planned."

The ex-sergeant pushed out his lower lip. "Aye, there's good reasonin' in that," he said thoughtfully. Seeing the troubled look on his wife's face he realised a diplomatic change of subject was in order. He'd retired early because of Mary's growing concerns about violence and the dangers of his job, even in the tranquil Shetlands. "She reads too many gruesome detective stories," he'd quietly complained to his colleagues at his farewell.

He asked Alan to introduce 'his young friends'. The ploy worked, as Mary was immediately distracted, asking questions about Australia just as her husband had anticipated.

Well plied with good strong tea and fresh scones with homemade blackberry jam, it was no great effort for Elizabeth to politely wait until her hostess' curiosity seemed satisfied before explaining to the former policeman what had particularly brought her to the village.

Rory McGregor shook his head. "Nae, lass, there's nae McKews in or around Boardastubble. And there's nae been for as long as I can remember."

Alan Munro nodded. "I couldn't recall any either, Rory, but I thought if anybody'd ken it'd be you."

Elizabeth did her best to mask her disappointment, asking curious questions about the history of the village and its surrounding area. Mary proved a more valuable source of knowledge than her husband in that regard.

"It's really ma mother you should talk tae," said Mary. "What I know I mostly learned from her. She'd..."

At that point there was a knock on the croft door. Rory opened it – on the step stood an old woman, perhaps a head shorter than him but near enough to the same weight. Her resemblance to Mary was easy to see, despite the difference in age and hair colour. Mary's was still auburn, while the new arrival wore a blue rinse that hadn't been fashionable for decades (if it ever truly was).

"Oh, hello Ella!" said Rory. "Come on in."

The lady in the blue dress and cardigan levered off an incongruous pair of bright yellow wellingtons on the boot bug by Rory's door after handing her son-in-law a large plastic box.

"Mind that, lad," she said. "I've brought ye a Dundee cake," she explained as she entered.

"Hi Mum!" called Mary. "Kettle's on – fresh pot of tea on its way!"

Rory introduced the guests already crowding the room. "This is ma mother-in-law, Ella Crosby. It's quite clear outside – shall we take some chairs out tae the back of the croft and have a bit more room?"

As they moved some light furniture, Q discreetly asked John B., "Did you *wish* for her to turn up, babe?"

"Not consciously, sweetheart." He grinned. "Maybe she's got her own sort of magic."

They both smiled, remembering three remarkable old sisters they'd befriended on Islay.

As everyone settled around the little wooden table Rory had set up, Ella was staring hard at Elizabeth. She hadn't yet heard the explanation of why the Australian couple were there when she suddenly said, "Surely you're a St. Clair, lass? Ye've got the eyes!"

Puzzled, Elizabeth replied, "Um… no, I don't think so – my name is McKew," and proceeded to explain the little she knew of her father's history.

Ella Crosby listened thoughtfully, not taking her eyes off the young Australian woman's face. At the end of the all too brief recount she shook her head. "He can call himself whitever he likes, but ye've got the eyes of Kevin St. Clair – and more o' his looks besides."

Her son-in-law creased his brow. "Would this Kevin be old Morag St. Clair's son?"

That drew an uncomfortable moment of silence from the old woman.

"Oh come on, Mum – dinna leave us all wonderin'! Whit's the unpleasant gossip?" prompted Mary, who knew how to read her mother's silences.

Ella sipped at her tea. A highly principled woman, she was torn between some moral distaste for the family (or at least the man) in question, and tact for her daughter's guest. In the end she thought, 'Well, the lassie did ask.'

"Kevin was raised by Morag, right enough," Ella conceded. "But he wasnae her son."

Eyebrows were raised around the table as the blue-haired woman told her story.

"The boy was sent tae Kenneth and Morag as a wee bairn. Sent over frae the Orkneys by some o' Kenneth's kin whit lived there. The bairn was the… *product* o' a young brother and sister. George and Elizabeth Sinclair, they were."

The Australian woman caught her breath slightly. Was this who she'd been named for? Her mother had never mentioned it – only that 'her name was the last thing they'd agreed on'.

Ella continued, not noticing the young woman's reaction. "Well, of course, the family was mortified at what the pair had done. Their father, old Henry Sinclair – there's a name wi' a history – split them up. Kept the son wi' him on the Mainland, somewhere near Kirkwall I think, while the lass was sent tae the old family property on Egilsay. He wouldnae allow the bairn tae be kept wi' either. Too great a shame tae be borne, it was said. So the wee one was sent here, tae old Henry's cousin Kenneth."

Mother Crosby shook her head. "Even after Kenneth passed away, when the boy was still wee, old Henry wouldnae hear o' him returnin' tae either parent. Tae gi' him his due, I believe he did provide for Morag an' the lad, right enough. And just as well, for young Kevin was a right handful growin' up."

"A bad lad?" asked John B., with a teasing wink to Q.

"Not bad, as such," admitted Rory. "I was at school wi' him for a bit. He wasnae *bad* of himself, as such, but he had a knack for getting' other yins tae get themselves intae trouble."

"He could talk the leg off an iron pot, and the pot wouldnae know it was gone," said Ella gruffly.

Mary looked a little uncomfortable. "Aye, he was certainly… a charmer," she said, getting a brief sideways look from her husband.

As if sparing her daughter an awkward moment, Ella ploughed on with her story. "I dinna know aboot that, but he was more than a handful for Morag. She was a match for him, ye ken, but it took it oot o' the poor old soul. I dinna think she was ower distressed when Kevin went off tae sea."

"He joined the Royal Navy?" asked John B.

Ella shook her head. "Too much discipline there for that yin. It was the merchant navy he went off wi'. Never seen nor heard from here again. Left old Morag tae quietly drift intae her declinin' years."

"Is she still alive?" asked Elizabeth, contemplating a chat with the woman who raised her father.

Rory and Ella exchanged looks before the retired policeman spoke. "Alive, aye… I don't think she'd be a great deal o' help tae you though. She's well on in years, and mostly in her own wee world noo. If, as you suggest, Kevin changed his name, I dinna think she's aware o' it."

"From what my mother told me, such as it was, it'd be right in character if he left his foster mother and never spoke to her again," observed Elizabeth tersely. "I can only assume he jumped ship when he got to Australia – maybe that's why he changed his name."

John B. squeezed his beloved's hand. "Do you want to see her and talk to her anyway, sweetheart? She is your great-aunt, at least."

"My foster-granny too, I guess. Is she still in the village, Mr. McGregor?"

"She had tae be… moved a few years ago. She was getting' tae be a danger tae herself, I'm afraid. There's a place in Edinburgh that looks after folk like her. Sinclair money has helped keep the place open over the years, so I think they look after her as a special case," explained Rory.

His wife added, a little archly, "I wouldnae be surprised if there was still a wee bit o' old Henry's money and influence at play there, either."

If Elizabeth was disappointed she didn't show it. As far as her research was concerned the old woman sounded like a dead end. But there was something Ella had said…

"Mrs. Crosby, you mentioned something about Henry Sinclair having a history?"

"Och, no so much him, lass, as his name. A long time ago it was – Henry Sinclair, or Prince Henry as he was called. I could tell you a wee bit, but you'd be better wi' a library," Ella replied.

The brunette nodded, and turning to Alan asked, "Would the place in Lerwick you mentioned have anything useful, do you think?"

Munro agreed that it might indeed.

The little group chatted a while longer, the discussion shifting gently back to places the visitors had been, around Australia and other parts of the world. None of the Shetlanders had travelled much, but they were interested in what was out there.

It was a pleasant way to while away an hour or two, but Rory had a wall to work on, and the guide wanted to take his charges on to Haroldswick. The Australians gave their sincere thanks for the hospitality and the information, both so freely given. After handshakes had been exchanged all round, Munro's vehicle was soon cruising north again on the A968.

Suitably sustained by scones and a most excellent Dundee cake, none of the three were in any hurry for lunch. Instead, they pottered about the

Heritage Centre contentedly for a while. Elizabeth made copious notes, while John B. and Alan discussed some of the displays in detail. Stewart had a long-time passion for history, and was impressed that despite his many visits to the Centre Munro was clearly enthused about the place.

 Much of the Centre was devoted to the crofting and fishing history of Unst, and the crafts and boats associated thereto. There were other elements to catch the visitors' attention though – John B. was interested in the island's role as a strategic lookout over the North Atlantic during both World Wars, while his beloved was drawn to the exhibits devoted to the history of Pictish and Viking settlement.

 Engrossed as she became in her notes though, McKew was still conscious of a little niggle at the back of her mind about Henry Sinclair. It wasn't until later that evening that she learned John B. was feeling the same uncomfortable sensation.

 The wizard had developed enough awareness of his unexpected abilities to recognise a warning. He just had no clue as to what of.

.o0o.

4 TAKING A STAKE

Olaf Jorgenson didn't need to work. He'd done so for over forty years. He'd worked hard, and saved his money. On retiring from his job in the Norwegian port town of Alesund he and his wife had moved to the picturesque village of Hellesylt up in the fjord country. He was happy to spend his days carving wooden ornaments, and his evenings reading a book by the fire.

His wife Freya was the problem. He still loved her dearly after thirty-two years, but Freya liked to chat. And now that he wasn't spending long days in the office or down at the dock, he was her preferred option for chatting to. Chatting *at*, he might have said with a discreet sigh.

In search of a few nights of peace and quiet per week, Olaf had taken on a job as the watchman at the *Sunnylven Folkemuseum*.

Much less expansive than the grand open-air *Norsk Folkemuseum* in Oslo, it was an attractive little building mostly given over to intricate and elegant wood carvings from across a great range of Scandinavian history. That was the other great attraction for Olaf, who delighted in regularly casting an enthusiast's eye over the exhibits.

The job wasn't onerous. He could walk the entirety of the Sunnylven museum's corridors in little over an hour, and that was at a gentle amble while he admired his favourite carvings. There were CCTV cameras at both the front and back doors, the images they captured being recorded and displayed on two screens in the little office that Olaf seldom used.

He much preferred to spend his hours on duty in one of the visitors' chairs in the main hall of the museum, a book in his hand, and by his side a thermos of hot chocolate with just a dash of local cloudberry vodka.

Even if he had been looking at the security screens this night, Olaf wouldn't have noticed the black van that pulled up near the rear door of the little museum. Its driver had many years of experience in circumventing security measures, and he knew precisely the range and limitations of this model camera that he'd checked out weeks earlier.

Horst Bader alighted from the front passenger seat of the van, remaining just out of range of the security camera. Over his shoulder was a dark canvas bag, and in his hand was a Luger 9mm automatic that he raised. With a single casual shot he destroyed the lens of the camera. A veteran of the old East German state security service – the Stasi – Bader was an excellent marksman.

His business partner, the van's driver Harold Worcester gave a small nod of approval as he got out of the vehicle.

If their employer, sitting silently in the rear of the van, was at all impressed there was no outward show of it. That didn't matter to the two professionals. Payment was the only recognition that truly mattered.

The two men approached the door quickly but quietly, their footsteps making only the softest of crunches on the light dusting of snow. They waited on either side of the doorway for a carefully counted two minutes, in case the sudden loss of CCTV feed was quickly investigated by a zealous guard.

Former Stasi operative Horst Bader stood a little more than medium height. As a younger man his build had been solid, but without the discipline of regular training and exercise his girth had expanded somewhat. His wavy hair was greying as rapidly as it was receding. It would be a match race to see if there was going to be any left to go uniformly silver.

It was hard to determine his age. His olive skin remained smooth, his only wrinkles being frown lines mostly obscured by grey stubble. The same stubble also hid the scar of what he'd swear was only a recurrent cold sore on Bader's very full top lip.

The German's gray-blue eyes were constantly on a slow scan, and hinted at perennial disappointment with the world. Now that he was no longer obliged to move sharply with 'correct military bearing', he allowed himself to walk with a relaxed, loose-limbed gait. It well disguised the fact that, if required, he could still move quickly and powerfully.

He'd known Harold Worcester when the latter had been on the staff of the UK consulate in East Berlin doubling as a 'cultural attaché' and a 'covert operative' (in which role the word 'doubling' was appropriate). When the two Germanys were unified both men thought it wise to seek new employment. Recognising each other's skills, and their networks of contacts on the darker side of the law, they set up a very discreet business providing the sort of services not found in the Yellow Pages.

Worcester looked a very different character to his partner. They were aged within a year of each other, but the Englishman looked a decade older. He stood well over six feet tall, was broad shouldered and narrow waisted.

A lush growth of light brown hair cascaded over his shoulders, belying the deep lines on his long pale face. Meticulously clean-shaven, his dark brown eyes were as piercingly still as his partner's were restless.

When he walked he did so with short, rapid steps, with a lean as though his shoulders could not quite keep up with his hips. Now he stood rigidly, his right shoulder not quite touching the museum wall as he watched the exit.

Satisfied that there was no sign of activity from behind the door the two men exchanged nods. Worcester stepped forward, taking a slim black leather case from an inside pocket of his long coat. From the case he extracted one of a number of small cunning tools of his own devising.

The museum door was secured by both a sturdy old deadlock of over fifty years' vintage, and its complicated new counterpart, installed only that year. Neither lasted more than a few moments against Worcester's practiced hand.

The tall Englishman pulled a small aerosol can of machine oil from

another of his capacious coat pockets. He carefully sprayed the length of
the door where it joined to the frame and waited a moment for the lubri-
cant to penetrate any potentially squeaky hinge. Then he pushed the door
open with a suede-gloved hand.

 Relaxing in his usual chair in the main hall at the centre of the building,
Olaf hunched his shoulders momentarily as a slight chill breeze passed
over him. He was engrossed in the book he was reading, a dystopian
novel of the type he usually found too depressing to enjoy, but the quality
of the writing in this instance had captured his attention. Had his mind
not been elsewhere, it would have occurred to him that the sudden draught
meant that a window or door had been opened. Indeed, that thought
would probably have struck him in a few moments anyway, had he lived
that long.

 Bader had walked soundlessly through the back room and along the
hallway. Framed by the arched entrance to the main hall, he'd raised the
Luger and fired before the watchman knew he was there. The 9mm bullet
drove through Olaf's right temple, the last words the reader was aware of:
'darkness fell'.

 Their employer had given clear instructions of what to look for and where
to find it, and indeed both men had checked and confirmed the details on
their earlier visit.

 In a glass case against the wall of the room directly opposite Jorgenson's
body was a length of carved wood, almost black with age. The ends had
worn away, but it was still half the height of an average man. The two
professionals looked at their objective with only mild interest. It didn't
look especially valuable. The sole claim to fame that the piece enjoyed
was that it was the oldest carved relic in the little museum.

 Indeed, nobody seemed quite sure of just how old it was, but it had been
prised from the depths of the ice of the Geiranger Fjord years before. The
most common description was 'Proto-Viking' because, while some of the
carved patterns were reminiscent of Viking art, the artifact was clearly
considerably older than 700 A.D.

Neither man so much as shrugged. Theirs was not to reason why.
Worcester once more employed a tool from his slim black case. A lock
clicked and the door of the glass case swung open.

It was Bader's gloved hand that retrieved the object from the metal brackets that held it on display. He wore leather in preference to his partner's
more elegant suede – thicker, more durable and practical he averred. Even
so, as he grasped the wood the German fancied for a moment that he felt
something like a small electric shock pass through the leather into his
palm. Automatically he checked for wires, but there was no sign of any
cunning security system they'd missed.

The Englishman's pockets didn't bulge – the coat was too immaculately
tailored for that – but their capacity and the range of their contents sometimes seemed uncanny, even to Horst Bader who knew well how meticulously Worcester prepared for every task. Now the tall man produced
from an outside pocket a square of white silk, which unfolded to be more
than adequate to wrap their prize.

His companion reached into the bag slung from his shoulder, and extracted a carved piece of dark wood. It wasn't indistinguishable from the
one just removed, but it would take more than a casual examination by an
expert eye to notice the differences.

The faux artifact was set into the metal brackets, the glass door closed,
and the little lock gently manipulated to click back into place.

The two men moved to another case, close enough to the watchman's
body to have a small spattering of blood on its side. Worcester again dealt
with the lock, and they removed another carving. This small panel was
a newer, gaudier piece that was a relic of a medieval church, some of the
carving inlaid with gold and precious stones. No replacement this time,
the panel was handled carefully but casually, tucked unwrapped into the
canvas bag.

The case was closed, but left unlocked. Bader's eyes did what seemed a
jittery dance about the hall, though he was in fact quite calm. The taller

man led the way out. The rear door was left slightly ajar, a little pile of drifting snow starting to build up on the threshold.

 The canvas bag was placed on a back seat, eliciting barely a glance from the silent employer. The decorated panel would find its way onto the black market that existed for such items, and the euros it would bring were a bonus for the hired killers, freely and casually given. The panel was a distraction for investigators, nothing more.

What mattered was the old object now wrapped in white silk. Few people in the world truly knew what it was. Its new possessor did though. Knew what it was, and what it was capable of.

Olaf Jorgenson would be only the first.

.o0o.

5 FAMILY, HISTORY

The weather on the day following the Unst trip was still pleasantly mild and clear. Elizabeth's interest had been well and truly piqued though, and she was now keen to explore the Hays Dock museum as soon as possible. She'd made that decision on the way back from the northern island, and advised Alan accordingly.

The guide was content to have the day off – they'd agreed to meet again the next morning. As he looked out of the window of his comfortable cottage, though, he did think to himself, 'Too nice a day tae be inside – there'll be too few like it soon enough.'

Perhaps that was why the museum was almost deserted. The Australian couple constituted two thirds of the entire visitor population for the day. The other third was a surprisingly familiar figure. Elizabeth recognised the face engrossed in a thick volume at the reference desk, and nudged her beau.

"That's the guy who gave the lecture for the Historical Society on Islay," she whispered, pointing discreetly.

"So it is. Cecil, wasn't it? Hmm… y'know he might be just the man to help answer some of your questions."

"He looks busy, babe."

"Sweetheart, I cannot imagine *any* man being too busy to try to help you."

"That's sweet, babe, if a little biased…"

Before Q could object, John B. had walked over and quietly introduced himself to the historian. They spoke softly for a few moments, Stewart explaining where they'd encountered each other before and Cecil explaining that he'd come to Lerwick to research some contentious theories of Viking migration. The wizard apologised for the interruption, then told briefly of Q's interest.

The older man's face broke into a huge grin. His unfortunately yellow teeth made the broad smile look rather like a big slice of Edam cheese. He beckoned the brunette over.

"Ms. McKew is it? I'm Cecil Munn. I understand you enjoyed my little presentation in Sron Dubh."

"Thank you, yes. Please, call me Elizabeth. Yes, I must admit, Mr. Munn, you inspired me to learn a lot more."

"A teacher can have no higher praise, dear lady! Now, your untidy young man here tells me that you're interested in 'Prince' Henry Sinclair."

Q bit down on a sharp riposte to the 'untidy' comment. It was undeniably true, especially in comparison to the dapper historian, but she was automatically defensive of the man she loved. Stewart himself seemed quite unfazed. It was, admittedly, not one of his nattiest purple t-shirts that he was wearing. The Rolling Stones logo was looking old and worn. Much like the band, really.

The wizard squeezed his beloved's hand and said, "I'll leave you to pick Mr. Munn's brain as much as he'll allow, pretty lady. I'll go explore the World War 2 exhibit. See if I can find something to share with Wilko since that's his field of interest. If you haven't turned up by the time I'm done there I'll head for the Viking display."

"Oh, I want to look at that, too! I'll see you there. Thanks, babe," said Q and kissed him warmly before pulling up a chair beside the still smiling Munn.

"Right, we'll make a start!" said Cecil enthusiastically.

It proved an enlightening hour or so for her. She quickly realised that

Cecil wasn't intentionally rude, just unwittingly impolite in the way of people too absorbed in their own interests to observe social niceties. A few nods and well-placed, "Wow! Really?" reactions were all that were required to keep him happily reeling off information. Fortunately Elizabeth could write just about as rapidly as he could speak - her trusty notebook was filling fast.

The St Clairs, or Sinclairs as many were later named, held powerful earldoms in Caithness & Orkneys. It was to the Orcadian family that Henry Sinclair was born in 1345. Reputed to be tall and strong, he could speak fluent Latin, Norse, and the dialect of the Lowland Scots. He became a Knight Templar and made no secret of his ambition for greatness.

Henry wanted nothing less than his own kingdom, and spoke so openly and brazenly about it that he was nicknamed 'Prince Henry'. A well educated, well travelled man, Sinclair had heard all the Norse tales of a land far west of Greenland.

It seemed he was as charismatic and convincing as he was ambitious. He persuaded two of his Venetian friends – Nicolo and Antonio Zeno, who had made vast profits from ship-building, to come to Orkney and join his grand venture to set up a new realm in this unexplored country.

Nicolo died after an initial exploratory journey to Greenland, but Antonio carried on and described events in long detailed letters to his family in Venice. These became known as the Zeno narratives and were eventually published in 1558.

Munn explained that according to these letters the adventurers fitted out a small fleet, and Antonio armed it with modern new Piero cannons that he brought from Venice.

In 1398, Henry, Antonio and three hundred would-be colonists sailed west in twelve ships. Zeno wrote that they eventually reached Newfoundland, and spent their first winter in Nova Scotia. In the spring of 1399 the colonists sailed down the coast looking for land on which to settle.

"This doesn't appear in a lot of history books," Elizabeth observed cautiously.

Munn smiled. "I'm afraid, dear lady, that many historians tend to be very resistant to accepting things which conflict with what they consider 'established facts'. It requires a great deal of evidence to sway some of my more intransigent colleagues. In this case, however, I personally am of the view that enough evidence exists for us to reconsider our views of the early European settlement of North America."

He explained that a boulder at Lake Memphremagog on the US/Canada border near Montreal was inadvertently overturned in recent years. The stone was found to be carved with an outline of the Sinclair coat of arms next to a fairly accurate map of the North American coastline. Across that same lake in a creek bed was found a stone carving which resembled the Rosslyn Apprentice Pillar.

"Rosslyn? That name's familiar," said Elizabeth.

"And rightly so. Rosslyn chapel, south of Edinburgh, is a beautifully, and uniquely decorated church. Among its most unique features are carvings depicting plants such as maize and aloe vera. Bear in mind, Ms. McKew, that these are native to North America, and the chapel was constructed by the Sinclairs in 1446."

"After Henry's departure…"

"And long before Columbus returned from his voyage of discovery. Yes. Fascinating, eh?"

Elizabeth was genuinely impressed. "So what happened to Henry's new kingdom?" she asked.

"Well, it's known from Zeno's writings that Henry and Antonio sailed back to the Orkneys in 1400, apparently to collect provisions or more colonists – it's not quite clear. Unfortunately others of Henry's clan were as ambitious as he was, but had turned their attention to more local objectives. King Henry IV of England attacked Orkney at the same time as the would-be monarch arrived home, and the English forces killed the 'Prince'. Enough of his crew was left to pass on some information – evidently the origin of the Rosslyn carvings, for instance. But no one knows what became of the colonists left behind. They may have starved, been massacred, or inter-married with the Indians and gradually disappeared from sight, just as 'Prince' Henry Sinclair's name has faded from the minds of all but the most assiduous, or specialist, researchers."

Cecil stretched and rocked back on his chair as his audience finished her note taking.

"Now," he said, "You also mentioned an interest in what's called 'Viking' history, and that is perhaps not a surprising co-incidence. The Sinclairs of Orkney claimed direct lineage from a line of Viking kings."

The family name St. Clair probably originated in Normandy, Munn explained. But in 1379 the father of the 'Prince', also a Sir Henry Sinclair, claimed the Earldom of Orkney as his birthright from his mother's family, and that the claim was granted by King Haakon VI of Norway, setting in train the conflict with the English crown that would eventually cost the next generation's Henry his life.

Cecil and Elizabeth agreed that this probably contributed significantly to Prince Henry being inspired by the stories of Viking exploration and his desire to undertake his own voyage.

Munn may have been a man who enjoyed the sound of his own voice, but there was no doubt of his knowledge of his subject, or his willingness to share. Elizabeth was really grateful, and thanked the man accordingly when he'd finished his explanation. The big yellow smile in response was genuine. He liked an appreciative audience.

As the brunette stood up they shook hands. It was an unusually tactile gesture from the historian, who ordinarily preferred not to touch or be touched by other people. But there was something charming about the young Australian woman, and a fascinating sparkle to her green eyes. He hoped the scruffy chap in the purple t-shirt appreciated her. (Of course he did - deeply.)

 In some evidence of which, as soon as Q walked into the exhibit devoted to old Norse goods and relics her beau looked up from the explanation on ship-building techniques he'd been reading, walked to her and threw his arms about her.

"Beautiful big smile on your face, pretty lady," he said. "I take it you've had a productive time of it."

 Enthusiastically returning the embrace she replied, "You bet! I think I've got writer's cramp, and I'm going to need a new notebook!"

 John B. stepped back and gestured expansively about. "I hope you've got *some* space left. I'm pretty sure some of this lot will be useful for your book."

"I'm sure you're right. Isn't it marvelous, some of the stuff you find in these little regional museums and galleries? Hidden treasures – they can be quite a shock!"

 Some five hundred kilometres east-northeast, grim faced police were taking notes in another little regional museum. The stolen panel had been a treasured religious icon in its day and in its way, but the murder of Olaf Jorgenson was rather more of a shock. The investigators, though, had no clue of who was responsible and even less idea of the real reason why.

.o0o.

6 FOOTBALL, VIOLENCE

John B. and Q decided to raise a glass or two to a successful day at the museum. Alan had recommended the *Royal Anne*, and it was a comfortable stroll from their room at the *Ernster*.

Munro had proved a reliable pundit. No surprise there. The *Hangman's Arms* was the only destination they'd visited that was in any way disappointing, and that was the fault of one patron, not the guide or the bar itself. The *Royal Anne* was unquestionably a more salubrious establishment, though.

They dined quite early. There was a football match being telecast in the front bar later that John B. admitted he was keen to see. Aware that she'd been setting much of the agenda for their recent travels although he'd never complained, Q was happy to indulge the idea. Not a football fan herself, she figured on spending the time reviewing her notes and developing ideas for the book that was starting to coalesce in her head.

They'd savoured an exquisite dish of pork belly, apple and fresh local scallops with a bottle of excellent English sparkling wine. The style was a proper *Methode Champenoise*, although the grapes and manufacture hailed from Sussex, not France. There was clearly a reason why English wines were winning awards and an increasingly glowing reputation.

The last mouthfuls of the not-quite-champagne were enthusiastically polished off just in time for the couple to move from the lounge to the front bar before the game started. It wasn't crowded and they were able to secure a table with a good view of the television.

Smiling contentedly, Elizabeth opened her notebooks: the burgeoning one she'd been toting around, and a new acquisition to be used for drafting the story itself. She wasn't sure how much of her family history would make it into the novel. Perhaps none. It was profoundly interesting in its own right, but it was leading her into some fascinating history that could be the basis for a rollicking story without having to air her own past.

Stewart strolled to the bar to order a good single malt for himself and a chardonnay for his beloved. While waiting he idly chatted to a few locals who'd come in to watch the game. Loyalties were divided, but there was a clear majority of preference for Partick Thistle, notwithstanding their garish orange jerseys. John B. was happy to be in that majority. He admitted to supporting two teams in Scotland: Berwick Rangers, and whoever was playing the 'other' Rangers from Glasgow, who just happened to be the opponents in this night's game.

Once the game got going the crowd became more boisterous, variously cheering or protesting the ebb and flow of play, and decrying every refereeing decision that didn't go 'their' way. John B. was happily right in the thick of it. Despite herself, Elizabeth started to pay more attention to the football than her notes. It was the simple raw emotion on display. It was *fun*.

It wasn't just to support John B. that she decided to ally her sympathies with Partick. She liked the jersey – it looked like something their old friend Wilko might wear playing golf.

She looked across the table at her beau, unable to resist a laugh as he growled animatedly at a blue-shirted Rangers forward sidestepping a Thistle defender.

"So this is your idea of a good time, is it babe?" she asked playfully.

He blinked at her. "Well, yeah. Have you never sat in a bar and gotten caught up in a game?"

After a moment's thought the brunette replied, "Actually, no. I didn't go to the pub with Sonny. Those lunchtime or after work drinks with you and the gang were a 'stolen pleasure'. But I could get the hang of it."

John B. grinned at her momentarily before flicking his gaze back to the TV screen and grimacing.

"Oooh – hang on, they're not allowed to do that, are they?" asked Q.

"Only if you're wearing a blue shirt."

"Ah." There was a pause before she eyed John B. shrewdly. "That's you having a go at the ref, isn't it? You don't like the team in blue."

"Well spotted, beloved." He leaned over and kissed her hair.

That brought a big smile to the brunette's face. "I know you're enjoying the game, but thank you for remembering I'm here."

"Sweetheart, you're unforgettable."

The little moment of romance was perhaps incongruous, but it was a good close game, and passions were in the air.

Several blocks away from the *Royal Anne*, down by the docks in the *Brigand*, the game was also arousing heated emotions, although none of a romantic kind. Basher Gurley, for instance, was loudly pounding the bar and declaring the injustice of many of the referee's decisions.

John B. would have been somewhat unhappy to realise that he and the ranting bully were on the same side. Not enough for the wizard to change his allegiance, but enough to be embarrassed.

Two crewmen from a little Norwegian fishing boat berthed nearby exchanged derisory looks. The man beating the counter near them was clearly a buffoon. They were hardly mental giants either, but their skipper valued discipline highly. A night in the *Brigand* was a treat to be appreciated but not over-indulged. Self-control was the most important attribute looked for in anyone who joined the crew of the *Svalgsay*.

Ossian Jamison, the barman at the *Brigand*, was much less indulgent of Gurley than Tam at the *Hangman's Arms*. The bar was much rougher, so Basher tended to have plenty of latitude anyway, but there were still some lines not to be crossed. And with each swiftly consumed lager the former RAF man's belligerence increased and he lurched closer to those lines.

The *Royal Anne*'s standards of decorum were considerably higher, although they were relaxed somewhat during football games. Not unreasonably, in the customers' collective opinion. One local girl was pushing those boundaries though. She'd been working her way through a steady succession of vodka and limes.

It seemed that the last one, or the one before, had nudged her over some threshold of self-control, as she quite suddenly transformed from interested spectator to loud and opinionated commentator. Even those who, like her, were cheering for the team in orange weren't safe from her slurred invective.

Two of her increasingly embarrassed companions were abused for not cheering loudly enough when Partick were awarded a free kick. She shrieked in annoyance when the kick was scuffed and the ball easily retrieved by the Rangers' goalkeeper.

"Daft bloody gowk! I could hae kicked that bloody better maself! And I'm a bloody lady!" she roared.

There were plenty in the bar who laughed at that. It was just unfortunate that the lass happened to be looking in the direction of the Australians' table, so it was their mirth she noticed.

"Hey! What're you two laughin' at?"

It looked for a moment like she might be spoiling for a fight. She moved to get off her stool – falling off it seemed a possibility. One of her friends quickly grabbed a shoulder to address her unsteady wobble.

John B. held up a placatory hand and said, "Just enjoying the game, mate. How about you do the same?"

Secured by her friend's grip, the girl swayed on her stool as she waved one irritated hand (the other wasn't letting go of the vodka). It looked increasingly likely she'd be ejected soon as she swore randomly at any and all, in the bar or on the screen.

Fed up with the distraction John B. quietly said, "I wish she'd keep her mouth shut while the game's on."

The belligerent lass was growling and grinding her teeth at the television when there was a sudden click. The stainless steel braces on those grinding teeth had accidentally locked together. She worked her jaw furiously for a few moments, making very strange sound effects to the discreet amusement of her friends – they'd seen this happen before.

With memories of those incidents prodding at the corners of her clouded mind, the girl quietened down. She had some dim recollection that if she relaxed the problem would fix itself. Eventually. At least she could open her mouth just enough to pour more vodka into it.

She did manage to still glare at the Australian couple. John B. made a great show of being impressed by something happening in the game, pointing enthusiastically at the television over the lass's shoulder. Quick on the uptake, his beloved played along with an appropriately similar reaction.

The drunken girl, still struggling with her dental silverware, was suitably distracted and turned to look at the screen and see what she'd missed. By the time she'd adjusted the focus of both her eyes and her concentration, she'd forgotten the moment of conflict and was absorbed in the match.

The last twenty minutes of the game were genuinely engrossing. The Glasgow Rangers launched wave after wave of attack, while the Thistle defence stood firm. The Partick goalkeeper especially was putting in a heroic performance.

At yet another fine save by that worthy young man, Basher Gurley flailed an enthusiastic fist. It caught his half full beer glass and sent it spinning to shatter on the *Brigand*'s hard floor. It wasn't his first to meet that fate.

"Gie us another yin!" he loudly demanded.

Ossian had his hands on his hips, an angry glint in his eyes. "No' on yer life. Ye can bugger off, Basher. Ah'll allow one glass as an accident, but ye're hammered. Get yersel' oot," the barman ordered bluntly.

"Will I hell! Gimme a bloody drink! Game's no over yet."

"Ah dinna give a toss. Ye're no getting' any mair tae drink here tonight. Go home!"

"I'll bloody go when I'm bloody ready!" shouted Gurley, fists clenched.

He leaned over the counter, waving one of those fists belligerently. The barman grabbed the threatening wrist and gave what looked like a lazy flick. Basher came crashing off his stool and hit the floor hard. It was entirely by luck that he didn't land on his own broken glass. Before he could finish hauling himself to his feet by using the stool for leverage, Jamison had vaulted the counter.

Shrewdly positioning himself behind the drunk, Ossian grabbed the collar of Gurley's coat in one hand and the waistband of his trousers in the other. He didn't quite lift Basher into the air, but was easily able to propel the squirming figure to, and out of the doorway with some force.

"Noo git yersel' home!" he shouted, standing in the portal with arms folded.

"Nae! Bugger ye! I'm gonna…" Gurley slurred as he stumbled vaguely upright.

"Ye're gonna do nowt but leave. That's if ye're thinkin' tae ever drink in this bar again."

"Ye cannae treat me like this! I'm a bloody war hero, ye ken!"

The barman was unmoved. "Aye, Basher, we've all heard. But d'ye ken, it doesnae gie ye licence tae be smashin' the glassware in ma bar. Away wi' ye!"

Ossian stepped back inside, pointedly shutting the door in Gurley's face. The drunk waved an angry fist, but had just enough sense to recognise a lost cause. He reeled away into the night, cursing and muttering about the disrespect shown "tae a man wha'd seen active bloody service, ye ken."

He lurched off along the waterfront. He was past making the effort of climbing the hill to the *Hangman's Arms* or the *Royal Anne*, not that he'd have had much chance of being served in either. Certainly he'd have not been welcome at the latter bar.

The mood there was light and jovial. Even the vodka-fuelled loud lassie had calmed down, now that the only effective thing she could do with her mouth was pour another drink into it. Losing the ability to yell seemed, curiously, to have softened her mood.

A late winning goal to Partick Thistle was the icing on the cake, and there was much convivial raising of glasses and slapping of backs both in celebration and commiseration. One such slap was just the right jolt to release the contrary dental architecture, but the atmosphere was so cheerful that the lass had lost all hankering for a row.

"I don't think I'd fancy it every night of the week, but thanks babe. That was fun," said Q, planting a happy kiss on John B.'s cheek as he leaned over to put a fresh glass of wine in front of her.

"You're more than welcome, pretty lady. I've watched a lot of games over the years, but never in better company."

That won him another kiss, which in turn won a number of approving looks and polite (if not quite sober) applause from some spectators who no longer had a game of football to watch. It was a good-hearted gesture, reflecting the bonhomie in the bar of the *Royal Anne*.

Such a spirit would have been totally lost on the mean-tempered Basher Gurley, still weaving a zigzag path along the waterfront. He was still railing at the world as he staggered.

"I'm a bloody war hero," was the regular thread of his ramblings, and it was that phrase that he slurred in the direction of the captain of the *Svalgsay*, who was en route to collect the rest of the fishing boat's crew.

The skipper, dressed all in black, took a cautious step back and softly replied, "Oh yes?"

"Aye. I bloody was. Bloody well am!"

Swaying unsteadily, Basher started to narrate his 'heroic' exploits in the Middle East. The captain showed no emotion. Gurley was oblivious, too drunk to even focus on the face he was ranting at.

There was no gun tucked into the captain's waistband – there had been no killing planned for tonight. But here was an opportunity presenting itself, almost *demanding* to be taken. The fishing knife carried routinely as a tool of the trade would have to suffice. Much slighter of build than the 'war hero', the captain would have had little chance in a fight. But there was no fight.

So swift was the movement that Basher Gurley didn't even know he was in peril before his blood was pouring onto the footpath from the slash across his belly. He didn't feel any pain, only surprise. He looked up in surprise as his knees started to buckle, and had it in mind to say, "Hey, I recognise you," when a second slash of the knife tore through his throat.

The captain didn't wait to watch Basher's last attempt at a breath, only kneeling briefly to wipe the weapon clean on the victim's own coat.

Now to collect the crew. Tonight's catch was once again the most important consideration. The blood of the drunken 'hero' on the black attire was a minor annoyance, but it wasn't obvious. Similar dark stains from slaughtered fish were an occupational hazard, anyway.

Somewhere in the Shetland ether, along with the shade of John 'Basher' Gurley, floated the words, "I wish he'd go to hell." That seemed likely.

.oOo.

7 GUILT EDGED

It would be fair to say that the killing of Basher Gurley provoked mixed emotions. On the one hand, his passing was not lamented by anyone who knew him, or had even only met him briefly. It was widely considered that it would significantly improve the life of his wife.

The woman in question didn't disagree, especially when the RAF pension she was entitled to as his widow started coming in. At last, there was a benefit to being Mrs. John Gurley without the abuse that her status had routinely entailed.

On the other hand, it was disconcerting to have a second unsolved murder on the island so soon after Colonel Hastings'. Not that there was any reason for anyone to connect the two.

Alan had expressed the two ends of the spectrum of feelings when he'd come to collect the Australians for a day trip to the 'far north'.

Muckle Flugga is regarded as the most northerly point of Great Britain, and much of the scenery en route to it is simply splendid, especially on a clear day such as this promised to be. They'd visited the northerly island of Unst on the day that they'd met the McGregors and Ella Crosby, but then their focus had been on history. It would do the island justice to spend some time taking in its spectacular natural attractions.

All of this the guide explained, yet without quite the enthusiasm the subject warranted, or that he normally would have shown. The murders were clearly preying on his mind.

Beyond agreeing that yes, it was a terrible thing, his guests chose to not discuss the matter further. It seemed the most diplomatic course to chart. They privately hoped that a day of close contact with an environment he clearly loved might be a good tonic for him.

There were effective distractions throughout their travel. They visited the Nature Reserve at the Keen of Hamar – an extraordinary, almost lunar landscape that at first sight looked like a bare sloping stony desert. It was only on closer examination, guided by Munro's practiced eye, that the visitors realised that the rocky debris was home to a variety of tough, low-growing plants.

"Worth seein' in spring," the guide said. "There's a lot come into flower then." Indicating one little patch of dark green leaves he explained, "This one wee chickweed isnae found anywhere else on Earth. Pretty wee white flower comes out in June. Oh! Aye! Here – look at this yin."

They all knelt to examine a small plant with tough leathery leaves, poking through the scree of gravel and thin grass.

"Is that – an orchid?" ventured Elizabeth.

"Aye Miss," said Alan proudly. "A bonny wee beauty it is. Called the frog orchid. It's so dry here that the flowers are much redder than the ones that grow down south."

John B. looked up at the sky. Although it was clear he couldn't help but remark, "I'm not sure 'dry' is a word I associate with the Shetlands, my friend!"

Munro laughed – the first time he'd done so that day. The strategy to ease his mind was starting to work.

"There's no a lack o' rain, right enough. But there's no the soil here tae hold it. All the water runs straight off tae the sea in summer. There'll be ice in winter, aye, but as soon as it melts it's away too. Fractures the bigger rocks, carries the smallest ones doon wi' the melt. It's what gives the Keen its look. *Hamar* just means 'rocks on the hillside', ye see."

Soon after, both Alan and Elizabeth averred that the view from one particular rugged cliff top was truly spectacular. John B. was happy to accept their assessment from a distance. He'd had his fill of steep cliffs recently.

There were scars (visible and otherwise) that would take a long time to heal.

He had been willing to approach a point from which the guide pointed across to the Muckle Flugga lighthouse, perched on a stack of ancient gneiss rock. The waves of the North Sea crashed around the building – it was undeniably breathtaking.

Later in the day, the couple rambled among the moorland of the Hermaness Nature Reserve watching birds wheeling overhead. Alan was showing signs of relaxing, staying in the car enjoying a good book as his clients took in the scenery and the clear bracing air.

They walked as they often did, each with an arm around the other's waist. They were a good fit.

"You're quiet, babe," said Q.

"Sorry, sweetheart. Thinking about Basher Gurley."

"Hmph. Not a pleasant subject at the best of times."

"True enough. I guess I'm just casting my mind back over anything I might have said. Worried that I, well…"

Elizabeth stopped their stroll and hugged her man tightly. "You listen to me, JB. That man was a violent, bloody awful bully. It's no surprise to me, and it shouldn't be to you, that someone finally had enough of him."

"Put him out of everyone's collective misery? Yeah, you're right, I suppose. It's just that this magic is so damned unpredictable, I worry that…"

"Babe, you do your best. You're a good man. The best I've ever known." She put her finger to his lips, silencing the protest he was about to make. "Yes, I've seen you fight, and I know you're capable of hurting someone. Very capable. But I don't believe you'd strike a blow physically or otherwise, in anything but defence. Of yourself, only maybe. Of someone else who needed it, yes, definitely."

"Of you, without a second thought."

She wrapped both arms around him. "Thank you. But this had nothing to do with you. A bad man got what he deserved. That's all."

Just barely Q stopped herself from adding, 'If you *did* have anything to do with it I'd be proud of you.' It was what she felt, but was perceptive enough to know that in his current frame of mind it wasn't the right thing to say. Self-doubt wasn't something she'd seen in Stewart before, and she realised the need to tread carefully.

John B. closed his eyes and leaned into her embrace. "Thus conscience doth make cowards of us all," he said softly.

"Cut your conscience some slack, babe. It's not like you've been deliberately malicious. Leave guilt for the guilty."

*

The new owner (or at least, possessor) of the *Sunnylven Folkemuseum*'s oldest artifact stepped from his motor launch. By Elizabeth McKew's reckoning he should have been feeling pangs of guilt, but that was a sensation he simply didn't know.

He'd seen the name Olaf Jorgenson in the newspaper report of the museum theft, but putting a name and description – 'devoted family man, wood carver and retired port office manager' – to the victim hadn't added a frisson of reaction. The guard had been an obstacle. Obstacles were to be removed. There was no question of right or wrong in his mind. The only question was: what was expedient?

The launch was secured at a small jetty, and was ordinarily the only link between the Norwegian coastline and this little private island. It was not much more than another rocky outcrop among several lying a scant ten kilometres from the mainland (although nearer to forty from Bergen, out past where the Hjelte Fjord opened into the North Sea).

All that particularly distinguished this island was its shape. It had a broad flat depression at its centre, the result of a tiny meteor strike millennia earlier. The result was a formation that had some resemblance to a volcano. The jagged spikes of rock that surrounded the central crater-like basin extended out in several directions into the sea like vicious teeth waiting to tear out the vitals of unsuspecting vessels. They'd given the small island its name of Svalgsay – 'the Swallower Island'.

The granite protrusions acted as a natural fence for the home that had been built at the island's heart. It was a simple utilitarian structure – a dome made of prefabricated fibre-reinforced polymer panels bolted together, and covered in earth and coarse, hardy grass.

Inside, light but tough fibreboard walls separated a small sleeping enclave and an all-purpose 'wet area' from the open living space that made up most of the circular residence. The furniture was for the most part basic but comfortable. The décor was more revelatory.

A series of low bookshelves were regularly spaced around the perimeter, perhaps an interior reflection of the stones encircling the outside of the dome. Each shelf was devoted exclusively to its own subject matter. There was no fiction on any of them.

At the due east and west points of the house's inner circumference stood identical chessboards, each of them occupied by a game in progress. From the walls hung a series of framed historical photographs, again evenly spaced in the gaps between the bookshelves.

Central to the round space stood a square teak table, ornately carved on its legs and sides with figures and symbols from Norse mythology. The top of the table was beautifully decorated with a fine piece of marquetry. It depicted the Nine Worlds, each stylized realm represented in a different fine timber veneer, all set off against a pine that was almost white. At the centre of the Nine – the centre of the table – was Midgard. The world of men was wrought in delicately cut ebony: a different wood but almost the same blackness as the ancient carved rod that was now laid carefully upon it.

Seemingly by instinct the man had placed it perfectly on the east-west axis of the house.

He pulled his favourite chair beside the table and settled onto it. The chair could hardly have been more different to the table. A polished stainless steel frame, with a profile that was vaguely swan-like, upholstered in soft black leather.

As he gazed at his prize his fingers unconsciously folded the fabric sheath that the artifact had been wrapped in by his two 'hired helpers'. The aesthetically minded Worcester may have appreciated the structure of the home. Bader would more likely approve of the simplicity of most of the furniture and décor.

Neither was ever likely to see the inside of this sanctum though. They had been brought to the island once when it was deemed necessary, but business had been conducted in the small courtyard outside the front door. This was the most private of properties. His relationship with the former espionage operatives was wholly and solely professional. Once he was confident that he had mastered the use of his new acquisition their services would no longer be required. Probably. Or perhaps some jobs may still be better done with a personal touch. Theirs of course, not his own.

.oOo.

8 IN THE QUIET OF THE NIGHT

John B. sat on a comfortable chair in a corner of their room in the *Ernster*. The light of the clock radio was enough to illuminate the form of his beloved Elizabeth, whose restless sleep had deposited her sprawled face down across the top of a tangle of sheets.

The same restlessness had roused him from his own slumber, and after several blows from flailing arms and knees he'd decided to vacate the bed until after the activity passed. That seemed to be happening gradually.

For now, though, he was content to simply sit, and watch.

His eyes followed the shape of her body, taking in every graceful line and curve. If he was an artist, he mused, he'd want to do justice to those curves.

How had it happened? At what splendid point had they turned from being workmates who enjoyed each other's company to… this?

Stewart had had lovers before. Had been in love before. He knew that the heavy drinking of his younger days had spoiled things. Knew that it had cost him what he thought at the time was the love of his life. He'd long carried a deeply buried burden of guilt for that, only recently finding the peace of mind to move on.

The magic, he pondered. For all of the strangeness that it had brought into his life, and the danger, it was still a gift.

Someone had angrily, sneeringly accused him of wanting to be 'a hero'. He really didn't. He had, he thought, a pretty well developed sense of right and wrong, and the magic had helped him to right, or prevent some wrongs. Some more serious than others. He didn't go looking for trouble, it just somehow seemed to find him.

But again he thought of the other side of the coin. The rewards. Never knowingly wished for, but gratefully accepted. A bank account that would keep him comfortable for many years, should he live so long. The freedom to leave unfulfilling work and to travel wherever he wanted. And best and most beautiful of all…

Q moved her arm slightly. Brunette curls fell about the base of her neck, brushing her shoulders like waves. The faint light glinted like whitecaps on her hair, enhancing the effect.

The curves of her body from behind – shoulders, back, waist, hips – did a view like this give someone the idea for the first violin, or something like it? He fought down the urge to go and wrap himself around her. She seemed to be sleeping more peacefully at last, and he didn't want to risk disturbing her.

'Where to from here?' he wondered to himself.

John B. Stewart had, as far back as he could remember, been unencumbered by ambition. Ask him what he wanted to be when he grew up, or in five years time, and he'd reply, "Happy." Pressed on what that actually meant he'd shrug and perhaps answer, "You just *know*, don't you?"

Now, 'happy' included leaving his immediate future in the capable hands of the green-eyed beauty sleeping before him. She wanted to write a novel, explore her family and ancestry – he'd go along with that, helping and supporting however he could.

There was no way of knowing where that would lead, or what it would lead to. But he'd given her his heart, why would he not entrust her with his destiny?

Q rolled over, her eyes open. Realising that he was sitting beside her, watching in the faint light, she smiled. It was a smile of love, and invitation.

He accepted.

.o0o.

9 FLOATING AN IDEA

Some considerable time later that morning, still basking in an afterglow of mutual contentment, the conversation between John B. and Q did actually turn to the specific question of, "Where to from here?"

"I think I'd like to go over to Norway."

"Uh-huh." He paused before continuing cautiously, "Arranging a flight isn't what you've got in mind, is it?"

Q snuggled in closer to his chest. "We-e-e-ll… I thought it might be exciting to sail over the way my ancestors used to go back and forth."

"We'd need a boat, and a crew."

"The size of the crew depends on the size of the boat. If we get the right little boat, we could do the journey ourselves. Just you and me. That'd be romantic," she said in a seductive purr, wriggling against him for emphasis.

"Sweetheart, as much as I love you, we both know that's not true. We'd be sleeping, and working, in shifts the whole time. I'm not saying we couldn't do the trip – probably, I think – remember I'm no sailor. But romantic, unless we happen to land on a deserted island paradise, no, not likely."

"Hmm, I guess you're right. But you'd do the trip with me anyway?"

"Of course. I'd go anywhere, and try anything with you, pretty lady."

She kissed him and wriggled even closer, looking for something else to try.

*

Sometime considerably later *again* that morning they'd just made it to the last serving of breakfast in the *Ernster*'s dining room.

In response to the phone call they'd made as they left their room, Alan arrived just as they were finishing the last of their potato scones and poached eggs. After availing himself of the offered coffee, the guide sat down at their table.

"Well, what have ye in mind?" he asked.

The couple exchanged looks – what would this canny man think? Would his local knowledge blow the grand idea out of the water (so to speak)? Elizabeth determinedly kept her enthusiasm in check as she explained their thought of somehow sailing from the Shetlands to Norway.

To his credit, Munro looked neither surprised nor skeptical. To his way of thinking, nobody sane would propose such a venture if they didn't have the requisite skills or experience. While this couple sometimes came across as a little strange, they certainly didn't seem crazy.

"It's no an easy task ye'd be undertakin' for yourselves. And I dinna just mean the sailin'. Would ye perhaps be better crewin' somebody else's boat that's makin' the trip anyway? A fishin' boat maybe?"

John B. shrugged but Elizabeth shook her head and said, "I'd rather not. I'd really like it to be *my* story. *Our* story."

That confirmed the guide's unvoiced hunch as to the source of this idea.

She continued, "Could we hire a boat, Alan?"

"Hmm… that'll be yer first hard task, I'm thinkin'. We might ask around here doon at the docks, and over at Scalloway…"

"Great! Can we have a go at that today, please?"

"Aye, Miss Elizabeth. I wouldnae get ma hopes up too high, mind."

John B. had been thoughtfully silent, seemingly deep in contemplation of his coffee. Looking up he said, "Sweetheart, if you're *that* determined, there's another option. If you can find the right boat, and I'll have to trust your judgement on that – we could buy it. Sail over in the wake of your ancestors, and then depending on what you want to do next, either sell it or sail on to parts unknown. Or should that be ports unknown?"

Munro and McKew both looked at him open mouthed at the suggestion. The guide had no idea that the scruffy Aussie was at all wealthy, yet he spoke of buying a boat as casually as if buying a new shirt.

The young woman obviously had a better idea of his situation, knowing of the existence of the Swiss bank account if not the detail of its worth. She was just taken aback at such casual generosity.

That was no reflection on John B. Stewart. But her ex-husband, and before that her mother, had no history of offering extravagant gifts. Any giving that was done had strings attached – sometimes nasty ones. With that thought in mind she really had to wrestle down the impulse to ask, "What's the catch?" She knew that if the question came out she'd want to kick herself. Everything that John B. said and did now bespoke nothing but genuine love for her. What she'd been through before, though…

Pat Benatar's *All Fired Up* was playing on the dining room radio. Elizabeth heard the lyric, "The deepest cuts are healed by faith," and bit her lip.

As she tried to untangle her thoughts, Alan Munro found his composure and said, "Aye, well, that might be more o' a possibility." He hastily added, "I still wouldnae get your hopes too high. There's no a lot of buyin' and sellin' o' boats here, and I'm thinkin' it'd be a pretty particular sort o' vessel you'd be requirin'."

"Not your specialty, mate?" asked Stewart cheerfully.

"More or less everybody on Shetland knows a bit about boats. Everybody over a certain age, I should probably say. But there's plenty folk know more than me. But at least I do know where tae find those folk!" he grinned.

Alan was as good as his word. Over the hours they spent walking the Lerwick waterfront (carefully sidestepping the area taped off with "Crime Scene" signage) he introduced the Australians to several sailors, chandlers and boat owners who were happy to discuss Elizabeth's ambition.

Yes, it was feasible. Boats crossed that part of the North Sea regularly, fishing boats as well as some quite small pleasure craft. Did they know that yon man from the television was intending to make the same crossing, on his own? No one knew of anybody with a suitable boat on the market. The absence of 'For Sale' signs on any boats wasn't as big a clue as Elizabeth was starting to fear, though, as much of what trade did exist was conducted solely by word of mouth.

Mid-afternoon saw the three of them sitting in front of a little waterfront café. Alan and Elizabeth sipped at cups of tea. John B. enjoyed one of the fluorescent orange soft drinks that his adoptive father had introduced him to years before. He was apparently oblivious to the falling temperature that prompted the others' choice of hot drinks.

"I'm sorry we've no had so much as a hint o' success, Miss," said Munro. "I did warn ye it might be difficult."

"Yes, you gave fair warning, Alan. No need to apologise. This was only our first day on the job – I'm not discouraged," Elizabeth reassured him.

"And tomorrow we can try Scalloway," said John B. "If there's no joy there, I'm sure Alan can keep his eyes and ears open for us. I know it's important to you sweetheart, but it's not like we're on a pressing timetable. Something will come along, and we'll be in the right place at the right time."

"I guess so, babe, but now I'm feeling really positive about doing the trip I just want to get on with it!"

*

The first hour or so of the next day's searching in Scalloway proved as

fruitless as their Lerwick effort. They decided to take a break and revital-
ize with coffee.

 As they strolled along the strand John B. stopped to examine a monu-
ment resembling a tall cairn topped with a bronze fishing boat. The others
joined him, Elizabeth reading over his shoulder the explanatory plaque
detailing the history of the 'Shetland Bus'. As they walked on, Alan filled
in details.

"Aye, in its early days it was entirely a civilian operation. The fishing
crews that plied their trade between here and the likes o' Bergen and
Alesund were rescuin' escaped prisoners and stranded soldiers from under
the noses o' the Germans occupyin' Norway. Mostly at night tae make it
harder for the Luftwaffe and the German patrol boats tae spot them. They
were pretty much unarmed, ye ken."

 John B. nodded. "So that's why the British Navy got a bit involved," he
said, recalling some of the information on the memorial.

"Passin' on information, providin' radios and light machine guns tae hide
on board. Eventually they took command o' it, made it a proper Operation, wi' headquarters in a big hoos in Lunna Ness, just out o' Lerwick.
But Scalloway was ever the real heart o' it, so they put a workshop and
accommodation and such back here."

"In five years there were nearly two hundred trips. More than a hundred o'
them were by the three 'submarine chaser' boats they got frae the Ameri-
cans and gave tae the Norwegian Navy, but a lot o' the workload was frae
the fishing fleet, just paekin' awa, one wee job at a time."

 This resolute pecking away at the German Navy was the story that Elizabeth had long ago seen on the TV documentary that gave her some small
inkling of her father. Fascinated, not least because of her growing appreci-
ation of local history, she said, "The memorial listed quite a few deaths."

"Aye lass, forty-four o' them. And most were men o' the coast, like all the
lads who were involved."

"Lads?" asked the brunette.

Munro drew a deep breath. "Lads. Most in their twenties, and many younger. A lot o' the older chaps were already on active service by then, and it'd been left tae the boys o' the families tae try tae keep the business goin'. So it was them as took on the responsibility, as they saw it. Many had families, and certainly friends, at both ends o' the Bus an' saw it as a way tae play de widdie wi' the Germans in Norway."

"Pardon?" said Elizabeth, blinking.

John B. smiled and translated, "To stuff up the Germans' plans, my love. A noble ambition, and one they succeeded in I reckon."

"Quite a story," said the brunette.

"Aye, and one we're proud of," replied Alan, the emotion plain in his voice. "The sailors themsel's have pretty much all passed away – I think there may be an old chap or two in a home down south, and there might be a couple over in Norway. But there's a wee group o' service people fra' other, later wars wha get together every so often tae raise a glass. Call themsel's the Bussers s a gesture o' respect."

Stewart mimed the raising of a glass - his own gesture of respect.

As the threesome shared a smile, someone who was clearly a familiar figure to the tour guide approached them.

"Alan! Ir ye doin away no sae bad, ma friend?"

Munro snapped off a salute – slightly teasing but respectful. "Aye Captain. Ah'm well and in good spirits, thank ye. And yerself?"

The salute was returned with a friendly smile. "A'm livin an life tinkin."

Even John B., who was usually quick to grasp unfamiliar dialects and languages, was having to think hard to keep up with the conversation. His beloved was a bit behind him. Alan suddenly realised his companions were likely bewildered by what they were hearing and turned to apologise.

"I'm sorry folks – just an exchange o' pleasantries…"

"No problem Alan, we figured as much, hey babe?" replied Elizabeth.

"Aye. And no apologies necessary mate – this is your home, you're entitled to speak your own tongue," agreed John B. warmly.

The newcomer smiled. "They sound like Australian accents, if I'm not mistaken," he said, his own voice morphing into the more neutral accent of someone who'd travelled extensively and needed to be understood.

"No, you're not wrong," answered the wizard, extending a hand. "John B. Stewart, and this is my beloved, Elizabeth McKew."

The man who Munro had addressed as 'Captain' gave a firm handshake to both of the visitors.

"That's a charming way to be introduced, ma'am," he said with a bow.

Q's smile was warm and sincere as she said, "He can be quite the charmer, yes."

Alan made the formal introduction. "Russell Morvyn, formerly of Her Majesty's Royal Navy, now comfortably retired. Funny thing, we were just talkin' about the Bussers, and here's one o' them!"

"All the more honoured to meet you, sir," said Stewart, with feeling. "Where did you serve, if you don't mind my asking?"

"The Gulf War, back in 1990," Morvyn replied in a carefully toneless voice.

Stewart caught the lack of inflection and resolved to ask no more, but Elizabeth was still caught up in her interest in the Shetland Bus story.

"I imagine there's a few of you from that era," she said. "Is that what the Bussers chat about?"

The square jaw under the meticulously neat beard clenched just a little. "No, ma'am. We get together to talk about friends and colleagues, not past conflicts. It makes for much happier gatherings."

"I've just put my foot in my mouth up to about calf level, haven't I? I'm so sorry, Captain Morvyn. Absolutely no offence intended!"

Her contrition was so obvious and sincere that Russell couldn't help but smile and bow. Besides, he appreciated a pretty face, and Elizabeth's certainly was in that category.

"Your gracious apology is happily accepted, ma'am."

"Call me Elizabeth, please, Captain."

"As you wish. And I'm Russell. I've not held a rank for quite some time. But Alan – I'm not retired any more." Talking to Munro, his voice slipped back into a Shetland accent. "I've just got back fra the sooth, meetin' ma solicitor and accountant in Aberdeen. I'm noo a licensed second hand dealer in boats and other sailing craft."

Alan clapped his friend warmly on the shoulder, and then with a broad smile said, "There's a grand piece o' timing, ma friend! Ye'd be the man tae help ma friends here, far more so than I can."

While Munro explained their mission, Elizabeth quietly said to John B., "You know what Wilko would say, don't you babe?"

"Something about a walking improbability field, I imagine," answered her boyfriend with a smile.

The brunette added some more details to their guide's explanation. Russell's brow creased in thought. Finally he folded his arms.

"Can you leave this with me for a day or two? I've a few thoughts in mind, but I need to talk to some folk. Alan, dunna sae clowe tae owt, aye?"

"I won't mention your involvement to anyone, Russell, but there's a few here, and more in Lerwick, who we've already spoken to."

"No matter. My approach may be a little different," the Navy veteran replied with a smile. With another courteous bow he took his leave, having noted down the contact details for his new clients.

'He's a man who finds a way to get a job done,' thought Elizabeth, recognising a kindred spirit.

Alan Munro rubbed his hands together. "Well then folks, would ye like tae have a wee while longer tae look around Scalloway? Oh, and I've had the thought o' somewhere ye might want tae have a look at on the way back tae Lerwick, Miss Elizabeth. Did ye notice the standing stone out on the road by the Loch o' Tingwall?"

"The Tingwall Stone you called it, didn't you Alan? Hard to miss, as big as it is and standing all alone there."

"Aye Miss. Well, it has another name – the Murder Stone. And it occurs tae me there's a connection tae your family history."

"Someone from my family was murdered there?" she asked.

"Er, no. But it's said the Lord of Skaldale, Malise Sperra, was killed there around 1390 in a dispute wi' his cousin. None other than Henry Sinclair, First Earl of Orkney. The old kirk in Tingwall, where the new one is now, was dedicated tae St. Magnus, and accordin' tae some stories there was a tower built there tae be the match o' the one the Sinclairs built at Egilsay, in the Orkneys. Not much there tae look at noo, I'm afraid, but if ye're interested?"

John B. looked at his darling, eyebrows raised in question. She smiled and squeezed his hand.

Gratefully she said, "There doesn't have to be much to actually see, Alan. Just to be in the place and soak up the atmosphere…"

"Feel the history, maybe see it in your mind's eye? Spoken like a writer, pretty lady," said the wizard. "That sounds like a good plan, Alan."

.oOo.

10 HUSTLE WITH RUSSELL

It was two days after the Australians had been introduced to Russell Mor-vyn. Elizabeth had spent much of the time writing, drawing inspiration from her copious notes and starting to craft a story as she built a fiction from the facts she'd been gathering.

John B. had engrossed himself in a few books he'd found on the *Ernster*'s shelves. They were mostly books about history and mythology, not all of it local. He also found two small useful instruction books – a beginner's guide to sailing and *Principles of Navigation*. Both of those were read intently from cover to cover.

As with many things that John B. Stewart read, they didn't feel so much like new knowledge as rediscovery of something lost. His own experience of sailing was minimal – he'd assisted with the return voyage on Bass Strait but was hardly at his best after his experiences on the tiny island of Mundara. He dreamed though. Ever since that fateful blow to the head there had been vague, dark visions in his sleep of time spent at sea. The details would vanish like morning mist when he woke, but they were there, somewhere deep. When he read the instruction books little flashes of familiarity went off in his brain. They were enough to give him some confidence that he could be more than ballast for his beloved Q's enterprise.

The pair had enjoyed one whole day sitting outside on the patio of the guesthouse, breaking off from their literary immersions only to refill coffee mugs and supply themselves with sandwiches and/or shortbread. It was quite an overcast day, with a sea breeze that carried a portent of the rapidly approaching winter. The brunette was sensibly rugged up, but her lover's concession to the weather was to have borrowed a light fleecy sleeveless vest from her and toss it over one of his usual t-shirts.

Meanwhile the former Navy man had busied himself making phone calls and paying calls on people around the islands. It says much about the force of his personality that men who would ordinarily simply expect potential buyers to come to them (whatever their inconvenient location might be) were convinced to bring their boats to Scalloway for inspection.

Shrewdly, Russell realised that even if a boat didn't suit Elizabeth McKew's requirements he would then know its details, good and bad, for other potential customers.

When he telephoned the Australian woman mid-afternoon to advise that he'd identified a number of possibilities for her, and ask if she'd care to meet him in Scalloway at noon the next day, he took pains to make it clear that he couldn't guarantee that any of the boats would be suitable. He hadn't seen all of them yet, but was happy to offer his advice when they examined them together.

Elizabeth carefully kept her enthusiasm under control while talking to Russell, calmly organizing the time and place to meet, and discussing the sorts of things they would be considering. What features were essential, and what were merely desirable? How much wear and tear, and downright disrepair, was acceptable? Morvyn raised the question of a price range. John B. had quietly offered Q the equivalent of a blank cheque, but by nature and experience she would look for value – a quite different thing to cheapness, and a distinction that Russell appreciated.

Once she'd put down the phone though, and started to convey the conversation to Stewart, her emotions began to bubble over. Eventually the wizard walked over to her, put a finger to her lips, then wrapped his arms around her and kissed her. Elizabeth savoured that for several moments before taking a deep breath and softly thanking him.

They retired to their room to give some tangible expression to their love. The business of talking business about boats would wait until later.

*

When they did meet up with Russell the next day – he kindly drove to Lerwick mid-morning to collect them – the couple had had their discussions about what to look for. As far as he was concerned, John B. contributed little beyond the willingness to pay. He'd learned a little, but Q was the one who would be running the show.

Over cups of tea at the *Ernster* the three had largely determined their approach. Russell would do much of the talking. He was familiar. He spoke the dialect preferred by many of Shetland's more senior sailors. And he was male. He didn't agree with the attitude, he stressed, but there were still some among the 'old hands' who couldn't accept that a woman could properly manage a boat.

Yes, young women had successfully circumnavigated the world in small boats. Yes, historically there were indications that Viking women sailed, and possibly commanded alongside their male counterparts. Yes, it was just stubbornness. But to get the best bargain from someone it may be necessary to tactfully manage his unreasonable views.

Stewart carefully suppressed a grin. He was quietly very impressed by Russell Morvyn's diplomatic prowess at resealing the can of worms he'd inadvertently opened.

They arrived at Scalloway bearing a list that Russell had compiled of who they were to meet, when, and where. He'd meticulously kept the potential sellers apart. It was inevitable that they'd chat – the community wasn't big – but he didn't want the 'products' displayed side by side. The Navy veteran believed that it would be hard for his clients (any clients), to not be influenced by comparative appearance, and he also know how misleading such appearances could be. The devil of a boat really was often in the detail.

As a carefully planned strategy, each of the three would play their own role in negotiations. Elizabeth (knowing she would often have to bite her tongue) was the bright-eyed would-be buyer with more enthusiasm than experience. John B. was the indulgent boyfriend who would presumably be taking out the loan to buy whatever boat was chosen, relying totally on the judgement of his sweetheart and their broker.

And their broker, ah yes, Russell – the well respected local who would *of course* be seen to be doing right by his clients, but could really be relied upon to put the interests of his fellow Shetlanders first. In reality the two Australians had greater faith in him than that. They'd decided that the former Captain was not a man who'd cheat either party to a deal he negotiated.

The first prospect they saw was never going to meet their requirements. Frankly, it seemed a small miracle the weather-beaten craft had made it to Scalloway from the northern island its owner called home.

Safely out of that owner's earshot Russell had muttered, "Joost a rattle a hellery…"

"Aye, but a piece o' junk that's been alright in her day," agreed John B.

"Still an on, tha day's been long past," said the broker, who then suddenly realised his client was picking up the local dialect.

Q laughed to herself. 'How *does* he do it?' she wondered.

Boat Number Two was in considerably better condition. It was a largish fishing boat, only recently retired. There were some patches and obvious rough repairs, but she seemed serviceable enough. It was debatable, though, whether she could be safely handled by a crew of two. The prospective seller was particularly dubious about this prospect with the realization that one of the crew would be the woman at the table. Pretty, sure, but not built to handle a working man's vessel like his.

Under the table John B. kept a restraining hand on his beloved's knee, willing her to remember her 'role'. Elizabeth was a model of restraint as Russell nodded sagely at the old fisherman's concerns even as he pointed out that there were women skippering boats that plied the very sea-route he'd worked for years.

As the grizzled old fellow left Morvyn turned apologetically to the brunette.

"Sorry, Miss Elizabeth. Dir a want aboot him, I'm faird," he said quietly.

After a whispered comment from John B. she smiled. "He's a bit of a stookie, aye?"

Russell laughed out loud – a cheery sound the Australians hadn't heard before.
"Aye. He's not very bright at all, I'm afraid!"

Number Two was a prospect, then, but none of the trio was especially enthusiastic.

The third boat viewed was as unlike the second as chalk from cheese. It was small and immaculate. Pretty to the point of having floral chintz curtains on the narrow little cabin windows. It would be difficult to fit a crew of *more* than two aboard her. As it was, John B. felt obliged to stay ashore while the owner showed Russell and Elizabeth around his 'little treasure'. That didn't take long.

At the mention of the price Elizabeth really had to struggle to maintain her façade of smiling naivety. But Russell's brow creased on her behalf and he suggested that the figure might be somewhat optimistic. The youngish seller shrugged. If the broker had heard the right gossip, there was a forthcoming divorce to be paid for and there wasn't likely to be much compromise.

Still, as he later explained to his two clients, he'd have recommended against the boat anyway.

"She's a lemm laalie," he said over coffee. "A china toy – pretty but worthless. Fine enough to hug the coastline, or potter from one island to another on a good day, but the first big storm or rough sea she's caught in is likely to be her last."

Elizabeth agreed. "She struck me as too lightweight for the trip. Not a deep enough keel to be secure in heavy conditions, but not the shallow draft of the old longboats that skimmed the surface, either."

Impressed, Russell nodded approvingly. John B. said nothing. He just drank his coffee and waited for their next prospect to arrive.

It was a longer wait than expected. Boat Number Four didn't appear. Eventually, after an irritated phone call, Russell learned that the owner had been pressured by his wife to sell the boat to her brother, and in his consternation he hadn't thought to advise the broker.

"Sounds like a poor wheeflication to me... sorry – an excuse," grumbled Morvyn.

"Well, if it *is* true, I'd bet that he doesn't get the price from his brother-in-law he might have had from us," observed Stewart, comforting the other two somewhat.

The extended break allowed time for a more leisurely lunch than they'd expected before the fifth boat on their list pulled in to dock.

"There she is," said Russell, pointing out the window of the waterfront bar he'd recommended. It was in the *Sailors Rest*, which was the same hotel where the Bussers met in the comfortable lounge at the rear of the building.

Elizabeth's eyes widened, and she nudged her beau in the ribs.

"Do you recognise it?" she asked.

"Er... it's a boat," Stewart replied cautiously.

"It's an S & S 34. Remember the *Helen Back*? Mundara?"

Q and Wilko had hired just such a boat with which to rescue John B. when he'd been held captive on that small island in Bass Strait.

"Ah. I remember the trip back, but not a lot about the boat. I wasn't entirely with it, remember."

The wizard had been subjected to experiments that came perilously close to frying his brain. His rescue had come about just in time.

"It's an excellent model," said Russell, not catching his clients' conversation.

"I know – I've sailed one in Bass Strait. They're as good as their reputation," replied the brunette.

The ex-captain looked at her with new respect. Bass Strait was a notoriously difficult stretch of water. He cautiously enquired how big the crew had been, probing whether the woman's experience was the match of her enthusiasm.

"Just the three of us," she explained.

"Two and a bit, let's be honest, pretty lady. I wasn't much better than cargo on that trip," admitted Stewart. "Although I reckon I can be more useful this time," he hastened to add.

Inspecting the vessel brought some creased brows and concerned mutterings at first.

"She's become a bit o' a possack, Ah'm faird. Ah've nae had th' heart tae snug her since ma lassie died," admitted the greying owner.

"I'm afraid Bruce is right. She is rather a dog's breakfast," said Russell apologetically.

"But that's just cosmetic. Not hard for us to tidy her up where he hasn't," replied John B. "Is she structurally sound?"

"Ach aye, she's fendy!" averred the widower Bruce.

"Seaworthy," translated Russell in response to Elizabeth's questioning look.

They intensified their inspection, Elizabeth's green eyes flashing with enthusiasm as she slipped out of her ingénue character. Bruce thought nothing of this. His late wife had loved the sea and he simply accepted that the Australian woman was cut from similar cloth.

It was only with some difficulty that Russell quietly prevented his clients from agreeing on the purchase immediately.

"We do have one more boat to look at," he reminded them.

"This one's a hard act to follow."

"Aye, Mr. Stewart, but both courtesy and good business mean we should consider all options."

Overhearing this, Bruce nodded. He respected Russell Morvyn's position, and was content to wait to hear from the broker later.

As it happened, the last of the boats on their list was also an S & S 34. At first glance she was in better condition than Bruce's vessel. Certainly the interior was neater. But Russell's keen eye noted little things like scorched marks in and around the motor, small tears in corners and around edges of sails.

Elizabeth was again playing her 'little woman' role, but shrewdly made a mental note of things like a little too much play in the wheel and signs of water seeping through some window seals.

Back in the hotel soon afterwards John B. observed that there was a significant difference between a boat being kept clean, and being well maintained.

"There were some ropes that were well frayed and needed replacing. I wouldn't like to trust them in a gale," he said.

The other two agreed. Russell, the courteous professional, contacted four of the prospective sellers and diplomatically turned them down (promising to keep looking for a suitable buyer on their behalf, now he knew what they were offering).

He was prepared to haggle with Bruce when he called him but John B. shook his head. The wizard appreciated the unspoken motivation behind the sale, and the price being asked was reasonable. Elizabeth didn't argue. She was too grateful and excited to disagree.

One phone call later the deed was done. John B. would arrange a deposit in Russell's bank account, with the appropriate sum to then be forwarded to Bruce. The boat would be returned to Scalloway in a couple of days after being stripped of any personal belongings, and the broker undertook to get Bruce home to a coastal village at the north of the island.

John B. looked at the copious notes that Q had written about their new acquisition. He squeezed her hand and said; "Now there's a nice coincidence. Did you ever see the movie *High Society*? There's a sailing scene where Bing Crosby and Grace Kelly are on the little yacht, on their honeymoon. The boat and the song – both called *True Love*. This boat's name – the *Fior Ghaol* – means exactly that."

Drawing a smile from their broker, Q planted a kiss on her boyfriend's cheek. "I'm not surprised by *any* coincidences around you, babe."

.o0o.

11 AN ARTICLE OF NOTE

The owner of the private island of Svalgsay idly turned the page of the newspaper he'd collected on the previous day's visit to the mainland.

Meticulously reading every item in the broadsheet, he'd reached an article about a well-known television personality who would soon be visiting Norway. The man in question was to be undertaking one of his famous 'adventures' for the camera. He'd be sailing single-handed from the Shetland Islands over to the Norwegian coast, supposedly on the track of the early Vikings.

The article appeared to have profiled the man called Miskwa Burns in considerable detail. In reality, the writer had been quite lazy and done little research on his own behalf. The fabric of the 'profile' had been lifted almost entirely from Burns' own press releases.

The most recent of these had been issued to promote his forthcoming new venture with a view to attracting more sponsorship from local businesses. To that information the journalist had added items gleaned from previous releases that had coincided with the release of one of Burns' *Tough Trails* specials on Norwegian television.

It seemed that the Man Of Action (as he was billed) hailed originally from Canada. He had developed his taste for adventure while serving in the 'Special Forces'. The article didn't make it clear whether he'd been a commando in the British armed forces, or a member of the US 'Green Berets'. Neither was it ever disclosed exactly where he'd seen action. Exciting but strictly covert operations were hinted at.

On leaving the service Burns had travelled the world, "staring down danger", eventually starting to film his own exploits. An American television executive had recognised the testosterone-fuelled potential in the sample tape that landed on his desk and given the 'go-ahead' to production of the first series.

As the executive had shrewdly picked, *Tough Trails* proved popular with a certain demographic, and the audiences were good enough to support a number of Burns' 'specials' each year.

In interview Miskwa spoke at length about his desire to inspire others through his 'survival skills', and with transparently false modesty played up the value of his military service.

"That sort of training is a sound investment in any young man's future," he'd apparently advised.

The owner of the dome house curled a well-formed lip as he read that. The article gave no detail about exactly when the TV star would be making his voyage. No matter. That information would surely be known in Shetland and could be obtained readily enough.

He looked over at the length of ancient black wood resting on the richly inlaid table and permitted himself a smile.

After first reading everything on the reverse page he tore a photograph of the intrepid Miskwa Burns from the newspaper. His long fingers did a meticulously neat job of the task. No ragged edges or inadvertent small rips.

He stared coldly at the slightly grainy features in the rectangle pinched between thumb and forefinger.

Quietly he addressed the picture. "No amount of training will secure your future from the power of the Odinspear."

.o0o.

12 BEHIND A GRATING MAN THERE STANDS...

Preparing the newly acquired *Fior Ghaol* for the journey was one thing. Food, water, fuel – no problems. Checking charts and safety equipment, no problems for the nautically experienced. The paperwork was another matter. The number and variety of forms required by the Shetland and Norwegian authorities were regarded by many North Sea sailors as no less vexing than the weather.

Fortunately the Australians had plenty of experience in the Public Service in their own country. Elizabeth in particular had a talent for what her boy-friend called 'administrivia'.

"You can make red tape disappear faster than any magic I could conjure," he'd observed.

As they stood waiting for a Customs form to be stamped, or signed, or filed – they weren't sure which – a young woman joined them in the little foyer. They realised that they'd noticed her in the *Hangman's Arms*.

"Hello," said Elizabeth cheerfully. The room was too small for a failure to communicate to be anything but rude.

"Hi. I'm Jayne. Jayne Wood," came the smiling reply.

"Elizabeth McKew. This is my darling, John B. Stewart."

Jayne couldn't help but notice the way the scruffy man in the purple shirt beamed at that introduction. 'Not been a couple for long,' she correctly surmised.

John B. bowed gallantly. "G'day Jayne," he said. Did we no' see you in the *Hangman* the other night?" The more time he spent listening to the local accent, the more he unconsciously mimicked it.

"Oh yes! You were there that night when the buck's party came in. And that horrible creep was there."

"Yeah, he was memorable for all the wrong reasons," agreed the wizard. "Still, he'll no' be bothering anyone else again."

"Oh yes, I heard! You never like to think of someone being murdered, but if I'm honest it doesn't surprise me that someone… *dealt* with him."

There was no sign of the lone clerk returning. Whatever was being done to Elizabeth's paperwork was evidently a challenge, so there was plenty of opportunity for pleasant conversation.

"The man who was with you that evening – I don't think he's your partner, forgive me if I'm wrong – do I know his face from the television?" asked Elizabeth.

Jayne laughed. "No, *definitely* not partner! No offense but… God forbid! Yes, you might well recognise him. Miskwa Burns, man of action, former commando and world's greatest adventurer, just ask him."

With a smile and a gesture of recognition the Australian woman said, "The *Tough Trails* series." Seeing John B.'s blank look she explained, "My ex-husband was a fan. Burns used to travel with a pneumatic blonde in the early shows, didn't he?"

"So I believe," said Jayne. "His girlfriend at the time, I think. The show's producers liked the eye candy, but in the end Miskwa didn't want to share the spotlight."

"So you're not her replacement," said Stewart positively, but with a smile. The young woman was certainly attractive enough. Her long brown hair was a few shades lighter than that of his beloved, and her pale blue eyes were as distinctive as Q's flashing green ones.

"Thank you, but no. My place is behind the lens, not in front of it. I'm supposed to just be the camera operator, but I seem to be production assistant and general dogsbody too. Hence being here, making sure we've got all the right permissions for his 'epic solo voyage in the footsteps of the Vikings'. Very wet footsteps, obviously."

As the Australian couple laughed Jayne asked, "Are you planning to sail too?"

Elizabeth nodded. "Much like you, funnily enough. I've been exploring my family history and discovered a big Viking connection. I'm writing a book, and I want to get a first hand feel for the voyage between here and Norway."

"You're not sailing a longship, are you?"

That got another laugh, although John B. worried that he might have seen a little light go on in Q's green eyes.

"No, we've got an S & S 34. I've had some experience with one of them, out on Bass Strait."

The cinematographer whistled. "That's a fair place to practice your sea-craft," she said approvingly.

"I gather this crossing has its share of challenges too," admitted Elizabeth. "We'll see what the weather's like. I'd *like* to sail the whole way, but I'm happy to use the engine."

"Sensible attitude. It's a much better passage than the trip from Scotland to the Orkneys, mind you. I'm glad we managed to convince Miskwa *that* wasn't appropriate for a solo effort. Supposedly solo, anyway."

"You don't want any other cowboys thinking, 'That's a good idea!' and trying to copy him," observed Stewart.

"Absolutely right," said Jayne. "Have you heard of the 'Swelkie'? It's a violent race that extends off the north end of the little island Stroma. It runs east or west depending on the tide, often with its own whirlpool. On bad days even large ships can get pushed off course as they hit the tide."

"And yet it sounds almost cute, the name 'Swelkie', doesn't it? Something a local would call a mischievous puppy," said Elizabeth with a smile.

John B. laughed. "Ironically sweetheart, I think the name comes from Old Norse. I've read about it – there's an old Viking legend that the whirlpool is caused by a sea witch under the water, turning a mill wheel to grind the salt that keeps the ocean salty."

As she nodded Jayne continued, "Miskwa might – *might* – be able to manage it with a bit of luck, but if some other poor silly sod tried to do the same trip and *didn't* have the same luck, or a back-up crew on call, it would all end very badly."

"Can't have that on the action man's conscience," said Stewart drily.

"I'm not sure he has one of those. Frankly, if he did he wouldn't take some of the foolhardy risks he does, with a wife and kids back home."

"Miskwa Burns has a family?" asked Elizabeth in surprise.

"Oh yes. Came along after the pneumatic blonde," Jayne replied, grinning at Elizabeth. "Never mentioned on screen of course. Doesn't fit the image. Ex-Special Forces, unquenchable thirst for adventure, you know. The loyal wife and little ones don't actually see all that much of him. If one of his *Tough Trails* were to actually claim him, well, let's say I don't think that their loss has crossed his mind."

"They'll have the DVDs to remember him by," said Elizabeth wryly.

"And the royalties," added John B.

As the three laughed the clerk finally reappeared from whatever back room he'd been sequestered in.

"You're all cleared tae go, ma'am," he said, handing the paperwork over to the Australian woman.

"Thanks. Your turn," she said, smiling and stepping back to allow Jayne to the desk.

"Thanks. Travel safely. I hope I see you again before we all take off," replied the camera jockey.

Stewart bowed again. "I hope so. Take care. And I wish that, whatever dramas Miskwa Burns gets into, you manage to stay safe."

"Thanks for that – I aim to try!" she answered with a grin.

Q gave the wizard's arm a grateful squeeze. She'd taken an immediate liking to Jayne Wood, and appreciated the protection she believed Stewart's magic offered. She might not understand it, but she accepted it and had come to value it.

None of them knew how it would be tested.

.o0o.

13 A FAREWELL BLAST

The *Fior Ghaol* was duly delivered, appropriately cleaned of any personal effects of Bruce and his late wife. Her Gaelic name was still emblazoned on her hull. Elizabeth and John B. decided to leave the name intact, although between themselves they took to calling the boat by her Anglicized name of *True Love*. The Australians busied themselves tidying her, adding a few personal touches, and carrying out the minor maintenance tasks that Bruce hadn't got around to.

All of which took a little over a week. With some reluctance the couple had moved out of the *Ernster* and into a serviced room in Scalloway. It was a block behind the *Sailors Rest* – the waterfront hotel that had become their regular haunt when not actively working on their new vessel. The *True Love* was berthed almost diagonally opposite the front bar.

They were pleased to see more of Jayne over those days. Moored nearby was the small but sturdy vessel of choice for Miskwa Burns' not-quite-solo voyage to Norway. The Action Man was being filmed talking earnestly to grizzled locals. Their responses, even the polite ones, would inevitably be edited out anyway, as nobody in the TV audience outside of the Shetlands was likely to decipher the accents.

He was also filmed putting final touches on his boat. Elizabeth suspected he was really putting the finishing touches to preparations made by Jayne, or someone else in the Support Team – a small group of professionals discreetly keeping a low profile on the island while they ensured that medical and mechanical help could quickly swing into service if required. Jayne had quietly reassured her new friends that there was a fast boat and a helicopter at either end of the voyage "in case Miskwa gets us into an emergency".

To be fair to the television star, while he did enjoy the luxury of a support staff, he really did do a lot of preparatory work himself. He'd legitimately looked after himself in his early solo adventures. There'd been a certain amount of luck in his survival in those days. Burns never publicly acknowledged that, of course, but he had developed a quite comprehensive 'to do' list before setting off on an adventure. It was just that he'd discovered the pleasure of somebody else taking care of the tedious stuff like admin and shopping.

Having a back-up team kept the network happy by protecting their investment. When the network executives were happy, the dollars kept coming and so Miskwa Burns was happy.

To underscore his military pedigree Burns had called his boat *Warfish*. It did not amuse him that some local wags kept surreptitiously painting a letter D in front of the name, reapplying it whenever the Action Man erased the offending character.

John B. and Elizabeth decided to have a small 'farewell to Shetland' event in the front bar of the *Sailors Rest* on the night before their departure. It was a select group of invitees: Alan Munro, Russell Morvyn, Rory and Mary McGregor (Ella Crosby declining because it was "too far fer an old lassie tae travel, ye ken"), and Jayne Wood.

Miskwa Burns invited himself to accompany Jayne. It was a public bar so he could hardly be refused entry. He announced that the *Warfish* would also be embarking next day, so Jayne was obliged to take some film of the little gathering. She apologised to the Australians that The Star would doubtless insist that editing make it look like the event had been staged as *his* farewell.

"No worries," said John B. casually as he raised a shot of single malt. "For us it's a social occasion. If he wants to make some sort of promotional event out of it then there's no skin off our noses. Even better if the network wants to put some money on the bar!"

"That's a good idea!" agreed Jayne. "Miskwa isn't about to reach into his own pocket for anyone else, but the producers have given me a bit of a budget."

The pretty photographer grinned, and went to the bar to organize a 'tab', taking great care to advise and point out who was allowed to buy drinks on this particular account. The room was quite full, with the number of regular locals swelled by the social event.

The subject of her film-making prowess remained blissfully oblivious, not that he would be likely to care anyway. He was in his element, he thought, talking Man talk with Men who'd seen active service. There were women in that category there too, and it hadn't registered with Burns that nobody of either gender wanted to talk about their own exploits. What mattered to him was that they listened to *his* stories. By happy circumstance, the 'farewell drinks' coincided with a gathering of the Bussers.

According to their advertised schedule, the veterans' social group should have been sitting down together in the lounge in a few minutes time. The area was set aside for their use, as it routinely was on such nights – the management of the *Sailors Rest* were rightly proud to be associated with the group.

Russell had politely introduced his old comrades to his new friends, and the Australian couple had warmly greeted them. It would be an honour and a pleasure to share a few drinks with them, Stewart had said, carefully not going overboard in his reactions.

Of course Jayne was included in the introductions, which was how Miskwa came to be aware of the background of some of the folks he was mingling with.

Those same folks had attracted someone else's interest, too. The skipper of the *Svalgsay* had paid particular attention to the small typewritten notice in the front window of the *Sailors Rest*. The date and time of the Bussers' get-together had been noted days earlier, and quietly acted on only a couple of hours ago.

One additional black rubbish bag had been added to the little pile that accumulated outside against the back wall of the lounge before the weekly 'cleanup'. The small collection of bags and boxes was alongside the large gas cylinder that fed the artificial fire used to warm the lounge. Unbeknownst to the skipper the gas had run out earlier than expected, and the cylinder wouldn't be replaced until the following afternoon. But while that would put a wrinkle in the plan, there was enough explosive in the bag to do plenty of damage in its own right. Maybe the whole hotel wouldn't burn, but it should be enough to kill anyone in the lounge when the moment came.

In the front bar Miskwa Burns was holding court in one corner, but the ranks of those interested in his stories were starting to thin. Burns realised it, and a rather petulant peevish note crept into his voice.

"Just has to be the centre of attention. There's a bit of the spoilt child to him, isn't there?" observed Elizabeth.

Jayne answered, "You know, he often reminds me of my brother."

"Oh, sorry! No offence meant!" said the green-eyed woman quickly.

"Oh, none taken," was the laughing reply. "My brother's a jerk. I don't get paid to put up with him, though. I don't think anyone *could* pay me enough to put up with Greg for two months!"

The women shared a grin. Like John B., Elizabeth had no siblings, and when she heard comments like Jayne's she was very comfortable with that situation.

Most of the Bussers had gathered together, ready to say a last 'bon voyage' and take their leave. John B. however took advantage of the moment to deliver a tray full of drinks to the group – a gesture of respect to them all. Led by Russell, glasses were graciously raised and a toast made to the *Fior Ghaol* and those who sailed in her.

Just as the last of those glasses was being drained there was a loud *whoomp* from the back of the hotel. The whole building seemed to jump. Glass shattered in windows and mirrors, plaster cracked and fell from the walls and ceiling of the front bar. The barmaid who'd been just about to walk into the lounge reeled back, singed and screaming.

"Everybody out!" came a shout from somewhere.

Years of experience and training evidenced themselves as the Bussers kept their heads and set about getting patrons and staff out the front door as calmly and quickly as possible. The bar manager insisted on checking that nobody was in the back half of the hotel, and found himself accompanied by Russell Morvyn and John B. Stewart.

The three took a room or two to check each, moving rapidly as flames took hold of the building's wooden framework. Russell shepherded the kitchen staff out. The manager, once satisfied there was no one in the rooms he'd selected, gathered up the most crucial of books and papers from the office, ducking out just in time as a burning lintel fell from the door frame and smoke belched down from the ceiling. The wizard had found an off duty barman who'd been stunned by a lump of ornamental ceiling plaster dislodged by the explosion. He lifted the man in a textbook fireman's carry (a move he'd seen in wrestling matches on TV) and raced for the front exit.

There was remarkably little chaos. Shetlanders aren't easily rattled. The likes of the Bussers and the ex-policeman McGregor even less so. Rory was one of those determinedly applying fire hoses to contain the blaze before the part-timers from the nearby Fire Station could be assembled to bring their equipment. Everyone maintained a safe distance. A few injuries were attended to. The most serious seemed to be those of the fellow John B. had carried out.

It seemed that the damage, while substantial, would be contained to the back of the *Sailors Rest*. It would be rebuilt. There was widespread relief that there had been no major casualties, no loss of life from whatever had caused the blast.

It was an initial assumption that there had been a malfunction in the gas line – after all, there was no reason to suspect anything more sinister. The two recent murders put dark thoughts in the minds of some, though. Rory McGregor and the two Australians were among that number.

A crowd had naturally gathered around the site of the drama. Out at the fringe of the crowd was a figure dressed in the heavy black of a fishing boat's crew. John B. happened to glance up and meet the blue eyes almost hidden under a thick woolen hat. At the locked gaze each felt the hairs on their necks raise.

The wizard looked into a face that showed no emotion, not concern, pity nor remorse. If there was any expression, it was disappointment.

The captain sensed something significant in the shaggy man in the purple t-shirt. Danger.

In the next moment the crowd had shifted, and they were lost to each other's view. The black-garbed figure slipped away, back to the *Svalgsay*. There would be other opportunities. These could be pondered at sea. Now was an opportune time to go fishing.

Police arrived along with the Fire Service. Questions were asked and statements were taken and suspicions began to arise. Unsolved homicides tend to do that.

Miskwa Burns answered all that was asked of him but as far as he was concerned, whatever had occurred had nothing to do with him. He quickly decided that this was an unwelcome distraction and that he and Jayne would be setting off as early as possible next day – just as soon as the light was good for filming. Whatever strange events may be going on around the Shetlands, he wanted no part of them. He had a show to make.

After finishing her interview with a policewoman Q took her beau aside and quietly asked, "I suppose we're going to stay and investigate this explosion? And those murders?"

Stewart frowned as he looked around. "Only if you're really keen to, sweetheart."

"Well, no babe – I'd rather not…"

 John B. hugged her. "No, this really has got nothing to do with us. We're not some odd Agatha Christie-type couple, compulsively poking our noses into things. Are we? You've got a book to research, pretty lady. We're going sailing!"

.o0o.

14 SEA, MONSTER

The voyage started if not sedately, at least comfortably. The sea was reasonably flat across the morning, and the wind was steady but consistent.

It was a good opportunity for Elizabeth and John B. to settle into a rhythm. The brunette coached her beau on some of the practicalities of sailing. His intensive 'book learning' was valuable, but there's nothing like the feel of ropes, sails, and wheel to quickly build a relationship with a boat – and the sea under it.

Some distance off shore they encountered a small pod of dolphins heading south towards warmer waters. As the glistening grey bodies danced in the bow wave for a few minutes, Q and John B. took the opportunity to simply hold hands and enjoy the spectacle. Such moments were few and brief. As Stewart had predicted, as a crew of only two they were simply too busy for much of the time to enjoy each other's company.

As she rechecked her charts later, Q sighed and remarked, "Sometimes I wonder how my esteemed ancestors made the journeys they did with no maps. I suppose a lot were simply lost. Set off and were never seen again."

"There's a legend in one of the books I was reading in the Ernster," replied John B. "I think the bloke's name was Sigurd the Longsighted. It was reckoned that he could see channels in the water, and spot a harbour on a coastline miles distant."

The tale had resonated with him as he thought of the big Hawaiian who'd befriended him. A man known commonly as Courtesy, a select few also knew him simply as the Navigator. Not all of those few were alive. Stewart shivered momentarily.

"Are you okay, babe? You went quiet there all of a sudden."

"Oh – sorry, pretty lady. Mind wandering. I shouldn't let it out on its own, it's only little."

The joke at his own expense won him a hug, a prize he would always treasure.

The wizard spent some time in the galley in the evening, preparing a pasta Bolognese. It was simple, hearty, warm, and not too difficult to eat in conditions that were slowly getting choppier.

Noticing the weather, John B. recalled some lines from something he'd read in the small library of the *Ernster*. Prompted by Q, who claimed a lack of concern at their warning nature, he recited:

> "The gales, ugly sons of the Ancient Screamer,
> Began to send the snow.
> The waves, storm-loving daughters of the sea,
> Nursed by the mountains' frost,
> Wove and ripped again the foam."

"Sounds delightful!" said Elizabeth wryly.

"And that was supposedly in the summer," explained her beau. "It was in a thing called the *Edda*, written by Snorri Sturluson around 1220, but the suggestion was that he was preserving those lines from a much earlier poem, describing a voyage from Greenland that went via the Shetlands."

"Well, that makes sense," agreed the brunette. "I've encountered some of Sturluson's work while I've been researching my book. I didn't memorize any of it though!"

"I hadn't quite intended to," replied John B. "I was just taken by the description of the waves as 'daughters of the sea' I guess. Made me think of you, pretty lady."

An hour after dinner Elizabeth went to bed (rather reluctantly, and on her own). The pair had agreed to each take two hour shifts overnight. The thinking was that a longer spell of sleep would be too hard to wake up from – well, to wake up and function usefully. A shorter nap wouldn't really provide enough refreshment. Before her sleeping John B. had taken the time to give her shoulders and neck a brief but intense massage.

"Oh my Lord that's good! I swear I can feel knots untying. Babe, you really are amazing," she sighed as the tension fell away from her muscles.

"Learned a few things from an old fella in Alice Springs a while back," explained the wizard. "I'm not in his class, but it should help you sleep."

"Mmm – I'd love to have you do some more massage, work over a few more muscles…"

"Not right now, pretty lady. I love the idea, but it's my turn to keep our little floating love-nest afloat."

Q was asleep by the time he'd finished speaking. He'd learned well.

The arrangement may not have been romantic, but it was effective. John B. did enough to keep the *True Love* securely on course. Elizabeth's sailing experience saw her take some active precautions against the deteriorating conditions. Near the end of her first two-hour spell, not far from midnight she tied a couple of reefs in the main and set a stay sail. She acted more from wariness than necessity.

The wind had certainly increased, but it was the state of the sea itself that was of greater concern. At times waves came at the boat from different directions in rapid, confusing succession. It made steering hard work, too hard for the 'autohelm' to be depended on, and both members of the crew were glad they hadn't decided on longer shifts.

It was a little short of six in the morning. The swell was now predominantly coming from the north west, pounding at the boat's stern and persistently pushing her to starboard. John B. had become increasingly aware of the hypnotic percussion of the waves. His eyelids were getting heavy. He pulled his mobile phone from the tough buoyant waterproof case he'd bought in Bergen, conscious of the possibility of dropping it overboard. To keep himself awake he'd started playing one of his favourite albums on the device.

To be honest, it was the *only* album he had loaded onto his phone. Stewart had long resisted owning a mobile, only acquiring it at his beloved's insistence. Perhaps stubbornly (Stewart still claimed to be a Luddite at heart) he described much of the technology of the device as 'a total bloody mystery'. Nonetheless, when Elizabeth had guided him through the process of adding music his first choice had been Mike Oldfield's *Tubular Bells*.

The music did its job, preventing the rookie helmsman from succumbing to sleep as he happily hummed along. On its second playing the album had again reached the section in which Viv Stanshall introduced the various instruments that Oldfield was playing. Stewart was echoing the sonorous tones of the narrator when Q suddenly appeared at his weary shoulder bearing a steaming mug of coffee. Immediately the wizard switched off the music – here was an even better option for staying awake!

"I added a dash of whisky, babe. I figured you've earned it."

John B.'s reply was a grateful smile and a kiss. Arm in arm the couple looked out over the water. They both had their 'sea legs' and were as comfortable as could be with the motion of the *True Love* on the pitching sea.

There would be occasional moments of silence as a large swell pulled water from under them before rearing up and lifting the stern. A quick adjustment of the wheel, the boat would slide down the back of the moving hill, and the silence would break with the wave. The water thundered by. The morning light caught the top of the waves as they ran ahead, the foam caps looking like the plumes of a closely packed cavalry charging off to battle.

The sun was only a little higher in the sky when the *True Love* was overtaken. The Australian couple had been sailing conservatively. No such caution entered the head of Miskwa Burns. After his departure had been delayed by some last-minute photo opportunities, setting up (i.e. bribing) some locals to play a small crowd of well-wishers farewelling him at the dock, he had steadily made up time. The *Warfish* may have been a small vessel, but she was robust. To give him his due, Burns was an excellent sailor. He could read the conditions well, and was less foolhardy than he often appeared.

Recognising the Australians' boat, Jayne waved cheerily from the stern where she was filming. She swung the camera and shot some footage of the larger boat as Burns passed them. She knew that it wouldn't make it to television, but rightly thought that her new friends would appreciate receiving a copy.

Aware that he now had an audience as well as a camera, Miskwa made a couple of quick adjustments to slow the speed of the *Warfish*.

"I'll just give these Aussies something to watch for a while, Woody," the TV star called back over his shoulder, typically ignoring the fact that she hated the nickname.

Many miles distant on the rocky lump called Svalgsay, a grainy newspaper photograph of the ex-Special Forces man lay on a beautifully inlaid table. A lean man dressed all in black clutched an ancient length of dark timber in his left hand. With the point of the fragment he traced a symbol in the air just above a very specific area of the table's design, while he spoke in a low, almost musical voice.

The words were a strange mix of ancient and modern. Prominent amongst them was a name: that of Hevring, one of nine giantess daughters of Aegir the sea-god. He was summoning the Riser.

Aboard the *Warfish* Burns insisted on removing his lifejacket and shirt so Jayne could film him 'handling the conditions' bare-chested. Wind in his hair, muscles rippling. The pretty woman with the camera sighed. It was not a sigh of unrequited lust, whatever Miskwa may have assumed.

The *True Love* was some way astern and off to port, but still close enough to see the 'performance' of the smaller boat's master. Elizabeth rolled her eyes.

"I feel so sorry for Jayne," she said. "At least she's getting paid to put up with him, I suppose."

"Hope she's getting danger money," John B. wryly replied.

Suddenly the sea directly off the stern of the *Warfish* seemed to boil. A column of water rose up, slightly to starboard of the small vessel. The Australians watched in helpless amazement as the water climbed higher and what looked like a fist formed at its apex.

No natural wave ever looked like this. Nor behaved like it. The column bent like a great arm and the fist smashed down, hammering directly onto the wheel of the *Warfish*.

The boat simply shattered. Miskwa Burns disappeared below the waves, never to be seen again. As the stern of the craft shot up under the impact Jayne was flung into the sea. To the enormous relief of the two watching she bobbed back up to the surface in moments, her life jacket easily bearing both her weight and that of the camera she still automatically clutched.

With Hevring the Riser having fulfilled her summons the column of water instantly dispersed back into the sea. Elizabeth and John B. didn't waste time questioning what they'd just witnessed, they just headed for the wreckage with all the speed they could muster.

The flotsam of the smaller boat was no threat to their hull, and with the passing of the weird phenomenon that had claimed Burns the seas became noticeably calmer. While Elizabeth held the wheel Stewart was able to toss a rope to Jayne. As he hauled her aboard the *True Love* she shook her head dazedly.

"What the hell happened?" she asked.

"You tell me and we'll both know," grunted the wizard. "That *thing* was like nothing I've ever seen before."

"Thing? What thing?"

Q and John B. exchanged glances. Whatever had risen up out of the sea had done so behind Jayne's back.

"Some sort of big wave," called Elizabeth from the helm. "Get Jayne dry, babe, and find some clothes to fit. Then see if you can raise that support team on the radio."

Stewart wrapped a towel around the photographer's shoulders. She was a little more voluptuous than his beloved, but track pants and a thick jumper over one of his own t-shirts should suffice.

"Any sign of Miskwa?" asked Jayne as she was gently guided below.

"The way your boat smashed, we were lucky to find *you*," said John B.

Jayne was silent for a moment while she collected herself. Then she forced a smile as she leaned into his comforting embrace. "It's a good thing that Wood floats, eh?"

The wizard smiled. This woman was a survivor.

On Svalgsay a puff of breath blew a charred fragment of newspaper off an ornate tabletop. The man who'd wielded the ancient magic betrayed no sign of the excitement he felt. A small smile of satisfaction was as much as he allowed himself.

There would be a report in the media soon enough, but the spontaneous destruction of Miskwa Burns' image was all the confirmation required to know that Hevring had been successful.

.o0o.

15 THE PAST CATCHES UP

Almost as though making up for the drama that had just occurred, the weather for the rest of the voyage was uncommonly favourable. The *True Love* made port in Bergen by mid-afternoon.

The support people provided by the television network were waiting for them at the dock. There were no other media present – the network team had managed to keep the story quiet for now. The Australians were happy to be kept right out of it. When a press release was finally issued it merely stated that: "Ms. Wood had fortunately been picked up by a passing vessel".

Proving her resilience, the photographer was entirely composed by the time they landed in Norway. Almost immediately she was organizing her support team to arrange new clothes and personal effects to replace what she'd lost at sea. The only hint of distress was her emphatic declaration that she wanted to "get back to Canada as quickly as possible, and by air, *not* sea, thank you!"

Having made sure that Jayne Wood was safely in the hands of her support team, and saying sincerely fond farewells, Elizabeth and John B. took care of their Arrival paperwork. That task was complicated by the requirement for them to submit a report on their observations of the demise of Miskwa Burns' vessel.

It seemed likely that describing what they'd *really* seen would only provoke disbelief and quite possibly draw suspicion onto themselves. While still at sea they'd concocted a story, talking it over with Jayne.

She genuinely hadn't seen anything. At the stern of the boat, she'd been behind her camera with a tight focus on the Action Man as he steered. The sudden impact of water from behind and above her had been the first inkling of danger.

'A strange freak wave,' wrote Elizabeth McKew, captain of the *True Love*. 'I felt a heavy swell roll rapidly under our boat. We were lifted sharply and our keel smacked into the water with considerable force. As I looked forward I saw the swell run ahead continuing to grow. Just as it neared the *Warfish* running approximately one third of a nautical mile ahead of us, the wave, by now perhaps fifteen feet high, suddenly broke. I can only conjecture that there was something below the surface that caused this, perhaps a ridge of rocks related to the small island some way off our port bow. The wave actually engulfed the boat.'

'The impact of the wave seemed to strike some way forward of amidships. It is difficult to be certain from my angle of observation, but it was only the prow that I saw rise up sharply from the water, and I realised immediately that the vessel had broken apart.'

She went on to explain how she had hastened to provide whatever assistance was possible, how she and her crewmate had found the young woman clinging to a piece of wreckage and brought her aboard. There had been no sign of the skipper of the *Warfish*, and they'd been shocked to learn from the survivor that he hadn't been wearing a life preserver of any sort.

They'd searched the floating debris as thoroughly as they could, but were also conscious of the need to get the young lady to shore and a proper medical examination as quickly as possible.

With the statement and all other required forms finally signed and accepted at the Harbour Master's Office, albeit with some bemused scratching of the head by the staff there, they made their way into Bergen. They'd left their bags on board the *True Love*. If necessary that would do as a place to rest until they found accommodation they liked, although they didn't expect that to be a problem.

"I wish we could find somewhere nice and 'homey' to stay," John B. had said as they disembarked. Now as they walked away from the dock area he said, "I don't know about you, pretty lady, but I reckon I could do with a drink."

Q squeezed his hand that she was holding. "You'll get no argument from me, babe."

They found a good bar along the waterfront. Good, welcoming, and expensive. Norway is one of the most expensive places in Europe, perhaps the world, for alcohol. The government levies a high tax on anything stronger than a mid-strength beer – an effective strategy, they hope, to raise revenue and curb excessive drinking.

Stewart didn't care. He withdrew a fistful of the local currency, *kroner*, from an ATM, ordered a beer and a single malt Scotch for himself and a very large glass of good French white wine for his beloved. They sat for a while in companionable silence. They savoured those drinks, and the round that followed, and let the stresses of the voyage recede like an ebbing tide.

Just as John B. was about to haul himself up from the comfortable low-slung chair and go buy them another round, he stopped and froze.

"What's wrong, babe? You look like you've seen a ghost!"

The wizard remained frozen, half out of his chair. "Not a ghost, pretty lady. Someone even more unlikely."

Green eyes followed his gaze across to the far side of the room. A big man was limping up to the bar, clearly hampered by his knees.

Well over six feet tall, solid rather than muscular. A bit like a taller version of JB's build, Elizabeth mused, but she preferred her bloke's deeper chest and narrower hips (features he'd apparently never noticed). Neat goatee beard, gold rimmed glasses, and most distinctive of all, a fawn broad brimmed felt hat. The man *had* to be Australian in that hat.

Seemingly having assured himself that his eyes weren't playing tricks on him, the wizard launched himself out of his chair. He stopped briefly to say, "Be right back," to the bemused brunette, then moved smartly (running was rarely his preferred option) across the room to where the man in the hat was about to order a beer.

John B. grasped the big fellow's arm. They looked at each other and in the same moment both said, "What the hell are *you* doing here?"

At which point they both started to laugh, and threw their arms around each other. The girl behind the bar coughed politely. She did have other customers to serve.

"Sir?" she asked.

The taller Australian asked for a beer, to which order Stewart added another round of what he and his beloved had been enjoying.

"Still on the good Scotch then, mate?"

"Developed a particular fondness for the Islay malts," John B. replied.

By this time the intrigue was too much for Elizabeth and she'd come over to join the men. With a grin from ear to ear her beau made the introductions.

"My darling Elizabeth McKew, meet Edmund Mapleton. My best mate back when I was at Uni, and quite probably the last bloke I'd expect to meet in a bar in Norway!"

Edmund immediately endeared himself to her by taking the hand she extended, bowing low and kissing the back of her fingers.

"I think you're only the second person to ever do that for me," she said.

"And I bet I can guess the first," answered Mapleton. His voice didn't boom, but it had a resonance that would be well suited to the stage.

"We've got a table over there if you'd like to join us," invited Elizabeth.

"I'd love to!"

As they crossed the bar room John B. and Q noticed how many people waved or called greetings to their unexpected companion. Clearly he was well known and well liked.

As they all sat she remarked casually, "No need for me to ask if you come here often. Is this your local?"

Edmund laughed. "Not exactly local, but I do usually drop in here whenever I come into town. At least once per fortnight. I play chess in the town hall on alternate Wednesdays. Today was business. Food bills to pay, for both the cows and the family," he said with a grin.

"Okay," said the wizard. "We clearly have some serious catching up to do. The last I knew, you were behind a Defence Department desk in Brisbane."

"And you'd gone off to Canberra. After a few phone calls and letters I lost track of where you were and what you were up to."

That comment left John B. looking genuinely contrite. "*Mea culpa,*" he said. "I'm not much of a correspondent, sorry. In truth, there wasn't much to report. I just got into a routine. Go to work, go to the bar, and go home. Nothing worth writing about."

"With this lovely lady? I find that hard to believe."

It was difficult not to like this man, Elizabeth mused as she said, "Oh, we're a recent development. We as an us, that is. We worked together for quite a while before things, well, changed."

"Like what?" asked Edmund.

Stewart answered first. "A while ago I hit my head on a poker machine. Pretty hard, I must admit…"

"Was there Scotch involved?" asked the man who clearly knew his old friend well.

"Yes, guilty as charged. Where it got weird though was that after that I found I could do magic. Make wishes that came true."

It struck Elizabeth that Edmund didn't seem to find anything odd, strange or crazy in that statement, as most people did. Including her, when she first heard it, she recalled.

Instead the big man asked casually, "And that's how you and Elizabeth got together? You wished…"

"No!" John B.'s response was emphatic. "I wouldn't…"

Q put her finger to his lips. "It's okay, babe. I know you never would. Hey, if anything, you're *my* wish come true." She kissed him gently before turning back to the smiling Edmund. "It's a bit complicated. I had a marriage that hadn't worked for a long while, and at the same time as I got out of that, I realised that I'd been working alongside the kindest, most caring man I've ever known. Some strange stuff happened along the way, but the important thing is, we're together now."

She went on to explain briefly why they'd travelled to the Shetlands then voyaged across to Bergen, carefully omitting details of the demise of Miskwa Burns.

At the end of her narration John B. raised his glass in acknowledgement and said, "So that's us in a rather large nutshell, old friend. Now, how did *you* come to be here? You mentioned cows, and a family."

"Family is how it all came about, really. My Mum's grandparents came from here, and when they passed away the farm went to her. She and Dad had no interest in it – Dad especially. The Army had been his life – even when he retired early he went to work for the Returned Servicemen's League. But I was interested. My Pop on Dad's side had been a cattle-man, and when I found out that there was that history on both sides, well, I figured it was in my blood. Even if it had skipped a generation! So I came up here to run the place."

"What did your family think of that?" asked Elizabeth.

"Oh, Mum and Dad thought I was mad. But I just knew it was the right thing for me. And I didn't have any other family to worry about back then."

"So your wife's a local girl."

"Only about as much as I am, John B. Local by adoption, I guess you'd call it. We met here in Bergen. There's a restaurant over the other side of town, near the art gallery. I went there on one of my first trips into town, and had absolutely the best beef wellington I'd ever eaten. I asked to say 'thanks' to the chef, and out from the kitchen came Anna. Working her way round the world from Florida. I told her how much I'd loved her food, we got to talking and, well, we still are. Two kids later."

That was the cue for the big man to pull the wallet from his pocket and show off the photo it contained. Anna's long blonde hair looked suitably Scandinavian, but her skin tone didn't quite match that impression. It was a few shades paler than the classic blonde Nordic, more the complexion of the fair-skinned red-haired image of Vikings. The children had their mother's skin and their father's dark hair.

"That's Ivy, and her brother Little Don," the proud father explained. "Hey! You've got to come out to the farm and meet them! Where are you staying?"

"Mate, we've literally just gotten off the boat. All our gear is still on board. We've made precisely zero plans."

"We've got plenty of room. You're welcome to stay with us!"

"Um, do you think you should run that past your wife first?" suggested Elizabeth, a woman who had experience of a husband who took her for granted.

Edmund waved a casual hand and replied, "Oh sure, I'll call her. But she'll say yes. I reckon she'll appreciate the company. We've got plenty of friends, but we don't get a lot of company. Now, let me buy a round of drinks."

As the big man limped to the bar Elizabeth leaned to her boyfriend and quietly said, "Somewhere 'homey' I think you wished for?"

He smiled back. "I hadn't been thinking of quite such a link with home. Old home. Are you okay with staying on a farm, sweetheart?"

"As long as we're together babe. It'll be a new experience, anyway."

They made that their last round of drinks, since Edmund was to drive. The farmer was sufficiently confident of Anne's welcome that he insisted that their luggage be collected from the boat and loaded into his wagon.

"I'll go get the bags, sweetheart," the wizard offered.

"I'm parked a couple of blocks the other way. How about I pick you up out the front of here?"

Elizabeth nodded. "That works. I'll go with JB - by the time we get to the *True Love* and back you should be here, right?"

A few minutes later as the couple walked hand in hand back towards their berth, Elizabeth quietly said, "I didn't like to ask – has Edmund always walked so… painfully?"

"I don't know if it's pain any more, or just sheer bloody stiffness. Before we met at Uni studying history, he'd been in Canberra at the military training college. His father's idea of a career for him. There was some sort of accident, I've never been quite sure what. But it stuffed up the cartilage in both of his knees. Well, either the accident or the surgery afterwards.

He never went into detail, but he couldn't watch M*A*S*H without making comments on 'meatball surgery'. I'm sure there must have been some sort of compensation – maybe the job in Defence after he had his degree was part of it. I doubt it would make up for crippling him for the rest of his life. Especially since at that age we didn't really think long term. He just got on with learning to live with it. Seems like he's managed."

"Poor bugger! Surely the cold here must make it worse."

Stewart shrugged. "The heat of Brisbane didn't seem to make it any better. Maybe nothing changes it much either way. It's been years, and Ed's what my Mum used to call 'not stubborn – *determined*'. Reckon he's gotten used to it."

They packed only a selection of clothes and belongings into a single bag: John B.'s trusty duffel. There was enough to keep them warm and allow a couple of changes, pending how things on the farm worked out. The *True Love* could be locked up quite securely.

The pair didn't hurry, knowing that their prospective host wouldn't be going at great speed either. The timing was just about perfect. The couple was waiting to cross the street to the bar when a bright yellow Volvo station wagon pulled up in front of them. Edmund gave a cheery wave from the driver's seat.

"Chuck your stuff in the back folks," he called. "Front seat's probably a bit more comfortable, Elizabeth, if you'd prefer."

The brunette accepted her boyfriend's chivalrous bow and sat herself alongside the driver. After maneuvering a Child Safety Capsule somewhat, John B. was able to squidge himself into the back seat behind her.

"Meet the Lemon," said Edmund.

"The name is just because of the colour, I hope," was Stewart's cautious response.

"Well, mostly. It *has* been known to struggle a bit on cold mornings," the driver grinned.

"Do you get many mornings that aren't cold?" asked Elizabeth wryly.

Mapleton laughed. "Nope. That's why I usually drive in the afternoon. Not that they're a lot warmer, especially coming in to this time of the year."

As they travelled, Edmund turned up the heater. A light flurry of snow was falling as they went over the top of the ridge that fringed the town. The ridge was really a ring of mountains – Bergen actually means 'the meadow among the mountains'.

They'd driven up one steep slope and were now cruising down the other side. It was perhaps a half hour journey, first out along a modest main road, then on something less. Edmund drove cautiously. He hadn't fitted chains to the tyres before leaving home and the conditions were starting to become a little treacherous.

The trip to the farm was completed without incident though. John B. volunteered to open the gate, an offer Edmund gratefully accepted. It was likewise welcomed when the wizard got out to open the door of the insulated barn where the Lemon was stored out of the weather.

As the wagon had crunched up the driveway Ivy and Little Don had run to stand just outside the door, ready to welcome their father home. They stared in puzzlement at the unfamiliar man and woman who accompanied him out of the barn. Daddy and the lady were sensibly wrapped up in coats and sweaters, but the man with the shaggy hair was only wearing a purple t-shirt and jeans. Even as young as they were, it seemed peculiar. Still, they were with Daddy, and he was home, and that was all that mattered.

"Hiya munchkins!" Edmund exclaimed as he approached. He threw his arms wide as both children ran and jumped into his embrace with excited squeals of "Daddy!!"

"Hi honey!" came a voice from inside the house, in an accent that had lost none of its American origins.

The farmer's practiced hand got the door open without losing any grip of the daughter tucked in his long arm.

They came into a good sized entry hall with a slate tiled floor, boot pegs angled out from the base of the walls on both sides, and a row of coat hooks also on each side wall. A range of colourful coats and parkas, both kids' and adults', already occupied half of those hooks. On the end hook hung a thick khaki greatcoat.

The alert green eyes of Elizabeth noted where insignias had once been sewn on the visible sleeve and shoulder of the coat, and she wondered momentarily at its history.

Such musings were cut short as they entered the large main living area and were greeted by Anna Mapleton, entering from the kitchen on their right. She'd seen the unexpected arrivals from the window by the stove where she happily spent a lot of her time. Her welcome was as warm as the house itself, and that basked in the glow of a wood burner in the centre of the living room. Her husband carried out the introductions. His delight in being reunited with his old friend was clear in his voice, while his joy in his family was equally evident to the visitors.

John B. dropped to his knees when being introduced to the kids, meeting them eye to eye at their level. It was an instinctive move, his experience with children was largely limited to having been one once, but it was a good one. Little Don, and especially Ivy immediately warmed to this shaggy friend of their father.

Anna led a tour of their home. The living room had a dining area set to one side, which also served as Edmund's office when required. In the centre of the room was the substantial firebox, flued up into the vaulted ceiling. It kept the whole house comfortably cozy. A large picture window, triple glazed of necessity, presented a splendid view. It looked out on an increasingly snow covered slope fringed with skeletal trees. In the fading light they were silhouettes against the white blanket.

John B. whistled in admiration, prompting a proud smile from his hosts.

"I'll show you around the property tomorrow," Edmund promised.

On the left of the main entry was the doorway to another small room, in effect a vestibule ringed with doors: to the main bedroom, a room for each of the children and a bathroom for them to share, and a guest bedroom.

"Yours for as long as you need it or want it," said Anna.

"Or until the kids drive you away," added Edmund playfully, scoring an equally playful pout from his daughter.

To Elizabeth's delight, 'their' room had its own ensuite, smaller than that off the main bedroom but more than adequate.

"Sorry about the mess. We use it as a storeroom mostly. Ed will clear some of it out for you, won't you sweetie?" It wasn't really a request.

"Sure. After dinner, okay? I could eat a horse…"

"And chase the jockey!" chimed in the voice of Little Don who was clearly learning his father's pet phrases by rote.

After a quick exchange of looks with Q the wizard patted his old friend's shoulder. "Absolutely no rush, mate. There's floor space for the bag, we can clear the bed to crash on when we need it. For tonight especially, that's all we need."

Satisfied that their guests were satisfied, Anna herded everyone back into the living room. She put a big pot of spiced and honey-sweetened red wine onto the firebox and passed out tin mugs to everyone. Even the kids, although their servings would be diluted by water from a small enamel jug.

The room was soothingly warm thanks to the heater.

"It's something you kind of build your life around for much of the year," admitted Anna.

Very soon Elizabeth had peeled off her sweater and black tights, and looked dressed for sub-tropical comfort in just a white tank top and a short sea green skirt made of something resembling leather. Edmund was happily married to a woman he openly considered the most beautiful in the world, but he did give his visitor an admiring glance. John B.'s gaze lingered a lot longer.

"Y'all have great legs, y'know that ma'am?"

"Why thank ya, kind sir."

Anna looked a little askance at the overdone accents, but was quickly reassured that they weren't making fun of her. It was simply a flirtatious habit that they'd fallen into soon after they'd first met.

"I think we both picked it up from the same cartoon when we were kids," Stewart suggested. "Never been able to take ma-a-agnolias seriously."

When John B. sat cross-legged on the floor, often his preferred posture, Ivy sat beside him. Her head was soon resting comfortably on his purple sleeve. Little Don sat on the couch between Edmund and Elizabeth, listening attentively to the chat that ensued between the adults.

Although ensconced back in the kitchen happily extending the evening's planned pasta meal to cater for the new arrivals, Anna was a keen participant. She'd been an enthusiastic traveller before unexpectedly settling down to be a farmer's wife. She'd been to the U.K., although not Islay or the northern islands. Australia had still been on her 'to do' list when she met and fell in love with her husband. Visiting his former home was still on that list.

To prevent any arguments they'd married in Norway, and helped the parents on both sides to fly to join them for the ceremony. It had been the last big trip for Anna's mother and Edmund's father. Both had passed away soon after the wedding, seemingly content with their offspring's future. Neither surviving parent had shown any inclination to again leave their warm climates, even for the lure of grandchildren.

"Maybe next year we'll sell a few cows and go off for a holiday to visit the folks," said Edmund casually.

"Sweetie, you've been saying that since we got married," said the voice from the kitchen.

"Yeah, but soon the kids will be big enough for a long flight."

"I already *am* a big girl!" came a protest.

"I'm big too!" followed close behind from the boy whose pet name indicated otherwise.

"Big enough to spend twenty hours on a plane without driving the other passengers crazy?" their father asked.

"Yes! Um… how much is twenty hours?" asked Little Don.

"That's nearly one whole day, isn't it Daddy?"

"Yes, Ivykins. From three hours before you get up in the morning to four hours after you're supposed to go to bed. And you'd have to sit and behave and be quiet for that whole time."

 Edmund smiled as he watched his children struggle to imagine that daunting prospect. Suddenly there was a sound like a small hinge that needed oiling. A small rather motley beige cat, evidently part Siamese, sauntered into the room from behind a long coat in the entry hall. It jumped up on the couch to sprawl across Edmund's lap.

"Hiya, squeaky," he said, jauntily rubbing the knuckles of one hand on the cat's head.

"Her real name is Marzipan, but Daddy calls her lots of other things," Ivy explained to her new friend John B.

"Including a few you're not supposed to repeat, I bet," he replied.

 That got a giggle from the girl, a guffaw from her father, and an equally loud laugh from her mother.

"Oh, you *do* know him well!" called Anna.

 They continued to chat about where they'd been and what they'd been up to in the years since the two men had last spoken to each other. John B.

left out a lot of detail of the dangers, natural and supernatural, that he and they had faced. 'Not in front of the children,' he figured. There'd be time for that later.

Then a cheery Florida voice called from the kitchen, "Now, wash hands everyone, ready for dinner!"

On his way to the dining table as he returned from the main bedroom, Edmund stopped at what Elizabeth had assumed to be a broom closet. Behind the long thin door turned out to be a carefully constructed space efficient wine rack.

"Much easier to insulate than the old stable where I used to keep 'em, and a lot less trouble than traipsing out through the snow in the dark," explained the grinning farmer as he brandished a good bottle of Rutherglen red.

The wine was an unexpected treat, and proved to be the ideal complement to excellent ravioli. By the end of the meal though, both Elizabeth and John B. were showing the effects of the rigours of the voyage. Their efforts as sailors, and the strain of dealing with – whatever had happened to the *Warfish*, and the subsequent rescue of Jayne, had taken a lot out of them. More than they'd let on, possibly even to themselves.

Edmund was blithely oblivious to the fact that he was carrying an increasingly large percentage of the conversation load on his own. It was his wife who said, "I think that there are four people at this table who should be in bed."

The children weren't too troubled. They knew it was past their bedtime. There'd be stories from their parents, who took it in turns to read to each.

The other pair in question didn't argue either. After bidding all four of their hosts a fond goodnight, they headed hand in hand for their bedroom.

"Wait! I've still got to clear the bed!" called Edmund.

The wizard waved his free hand. "Don't worry about it tonight, we'll be right," he called back as the couple half-staggered into the vestibule.

 Whatever was cluttering the bed could be moved to somewhere on the floor, or atop an existing pile until the morning. Doing that was the work of mere minutes. Shedding their outer layer of clothes took less time. There were barely enough moments for them to lie down, curled up in each other's arms, before sleep overwhelmed them.

.o0o.

16 OF COWS AND CHICKENS

Farm life started early, even in the Norwegian cold. The Mapletons had some difficulty convincing their kids that it *wouldn't* be a good idea to wake their guests so they could see the cows and help with the milking.

"They can meet the meat later," Edmund gravely intoned, a turn of phrase that Little Don gleefully parroted over and over a few hours later when the visitors did finally make it out to the dairy shed.

In the meantime they'd slept deeply, showered briskly, dressed, done a much neater job of tidying their room than they'd been able to manage the night before, and finally, as per the note Anna had left, helped themselves to two bowls of the oatmeal simmering gently on the stove.

Correctly they assumed that everyone was outside, with his or her own chores to do. The exception was Marzipan, who turned up from whatever hiding place she'd been occupying to sit purring at their feet as they ate at the dining table.

"Sorry kid, I'm not about to drop porridge on the floor for you," said John B.

The cat squeaked in apparent reply – it really was a most un-feline noise – and jumped up onto his lap. She seemed to know that climbing onto the table was a step too far, at least while anyone was watching. The wizard chuckled, shrugged, and put a dollop of his breakfast on the end of his finger. The cat's little pink tongue darted out and cleaned off the creamy blob.

Q tried the same thing, holding her hand out conveniently for the Siamese. Marzipan sniffed at the offering, ventured a small lick, but turned to look back up at her first feeder.

"Squeak."

"Oh, I see. My breakfast isn't good enough for you. Or perhaps you only play up to males," said Elizabeth in mock affront.

"You put a dash of maple syrup in your porridge. I think maybe she shares my preference for a pinch of salt," Stewart suggested.

"Hmm."

They finished the meal happily. The warmth in their bellies would be appreciated when they got outside. Across the course of the day they got a good tour of the property, and a good insight into its working.

"It's about sixteen hectares all up. We're lucky – most of that is useable. There are plenty of folks who don't get much value out of a bigger percentage of their land," explained Edmund. "We run between fifteen and twenty cattle at a time."

This was all news to Elizabeth. "You know, it never occurred to me that there was a dairy industry here. I suppose it's logical – I just didn't connect cows with Norway."

"Oh yeah, there are over 17000 dairy farms in the country. Even got our own breed, the Norwegian Red. Great cow. That's what these guys are." He slapped one beast affectionately on the rump. "We even export them to Ireland. Well, I don't. Not yet. Probably won't, to be honest. It'd mean expanding a lot and I don't really want to do that. I'd like to have some Jerseys, you get a much better price for their milk and you can actually run more per hectare. But we can't import live cattle into Norway, and a heifer in calf can cost over 2500 euros. That's a lot to gamble. And there's a two year waiting list anyway."

Together, Edmund and John B. forked out a last serving of grass onto the big feeding table in front of the cows. The table ran almost the width of the large shed that was the dairy.

Looking over at the row of stalls where the cows were milked twice daily Elizabeth asked, "You're not tempted to modernize a bit?"

"More than tempted sometimes. Especially in the early days when we were still getting used to the routine. I looked at spending a lot on automation, both feeding and milking, but in the end I calculated it wasn't worth the money. Especially when you factor in the interest I'd have to pay on the borrowing I'd need! The maths doesn't even come close to working out until you've got a much bigger herd. We don't have the land, and we don't want to invest any more time than we already do. Look, the profits aren't great, but we're ahead, we're comfortable, and we're happy."

"Can't ask for much more than that, hey? You know that even back in Roman times they knew about the dangers of over-investing in a farm? Pliny wrote *nihil minus expedire quam agram optime colere* – nothing pays worse than fancy farming," said Stewart. He knew that his old friend was good with figures, knew he'd have looked very closely at the costs, risks and benefits. If he thought it wasn't a wise investment, it pretty certainly wasn't.

Elizabeth was a little less sure, particularly concerned about her host's mobility issues. "As long as you're sure the workload is – sustainable," she said cautiously.

"Oh sure," was the airy reply. "Some days we work twenty hours, some days not much more than two. I manage a lot of it. Anna and the munchkins do their share, and as the kids get older they'll take more on."

"Assuming they want to."

The farmer grinned at Elizabeth's response. "So far so good. We have a hard time getting them off the farm jobs and into their lessons. We home school. It makes time management a bit easier. We've both got arts degrees. Anna planned to be a librarian before the cookery bug bit. Cooking's a more transportable skill for travelling the world with, too. But between us we're doing okay with teaching."

As he talked Edmund led the way to the farm's other substantial building. "Used to be the stable," he explained, "I was never much on horses, but."

He hustled his visitors inside quickly, opening and closing the door as fast

116

as he could. Small wooden crates were stacked against one wall, and a cool room had been built in a corner. Low shelves ran along the far wall. Straw lay abundantly across the floor. Anna and the children were rummaging amongst the straw, each of them carrying a wicker basket appropriate to the size of their arm.

"I got two! That makes eight – I lead!" cried Ivy, holding up a pair of substantial white eggs.

 Their eyes adjusting to the light, John B. and Elizabeth realised that scurrying about the floor of the old stable were a dozen or more chickens. Others roosted on or under the shelves. Most were dark brown, which had helped render them invisible in the low light. A few were cream, with bands that were almost yellow across their bodies. They weren't big birds, none was larger than a bantam.

"Wow! This place is the chook Hilton!" exclaimed John B.

"Hello!" called Anna. "Meet our other crop!"

"Chickens aren't a crop," said Little Don.

"No mate, but their eggs are a harvest," explained John B. with a smile.

"Too right, and a good one for us. These girls are great layers," said Edmund.

 Several of the birds trotted up to the big farmer, while some of the others continued to hang around Anne or the kids. Clearly most of them weren't bothered by human presence and some seemed to actually seek it out. One brown banded hen strode up to John B. and promptly sat down on his right foot, with a proprietary *cluck*.

After gathering the eggs that Ivy and Don had gathered into her own basket, Anna came over to stand beside her husband.

"They're called Jaerhons, a local breed," she explained. "Hardy little things, ideal for these conditions. They'll pretty much spend the winter in here, but we've got a big caged coop outside for when it's warmer."

"The cage is to keep foxes out," explained Ivy.

"Eagles too," added Anna. "Although by putting the cage under cover of a couple of trees we've cut down at least some of that danger."

The wizard squatted to pat the chicken on his foot. The hen accepted the touch quite placidly. "They lay just as well inside as out?" he asked.

"Pretty much," answered Anna. "If anything, that's the weakness of the breed. They produce so many eggs I think they wear themselves out. We have quite a steady turnover."

"Good eating," said Edmund. "And it teaches the kids not to get too attached to the animals."

"As endearing as they are," mused Elizabeth who was delighted to be following her boyfriend's example and scratching the back of a little cream hen who'd wandered up to investigate her. Patting a chicken was not something this city girl had ever contemplated, but it was actually quite a nice feeling. "So you have all the eggs you need," she observed.

"And then some!" said Edmund.

Anna smiled proudly. "I was serious when I called them our crop. During the warmer months I go down to the market once a week with crates of eggs. In winter I might go down once a month, just because the trip's more difficult, but I sell both fresh and frozen eggs then."

That drew a blank look from Elizabeth. "Frozen eggs?"

Again the farmer's wife smiled broadly. She beckoned them to follow her over to the cool room in the corner. She opened the door – not for long as none of them were dressed for the cold air of the room – and indicated row upon row of ice cube containers on shelves lining the walls.

"Orange ones for the beaten yolks – add a pinch of salt for every couple of eggs, stops the yolks being too thick to use when they thaw. White ones for the whites, of course," she explained, closing the cold room. "I used to just beat them all together and freeze the mix, but I found people were asking for the separate parts to cook with. It's really not much more difficult."

"And we get a better price for two bits than one whole egg!" added Edmund cheerily. "All additional income gratefully received!"

By mid-afternoon they were all settled back in the living room, enjoying the mulled wine that was again steaming gently on the firebox, and the view out the window. It hadn't actually snowed all day, but the air outside felt like a good fall wasn't far away. The light was already fading. The assistance of two willing and able bodies had allowed many of the days jobs to be completed much more quickly than usual.

For all of his claims of the business being in his blood, Edmund was a largely self-taught cattleman. A lot had been learned by trial and error before he'd managed to overcome some early mule-headedness and seek (and heed) some advice from locals.

At first, some of those locals had wondered what to make of the farm's new owners. Some already knew the young American woman from the restaurant, and appreciated that she could cook. But what did she know about running a farm? Her husband could be as bullish as some of the stock they possessed. But as he got better at listening before speaking they realised that he did, in fact, have a good eye for an animal.

They admired his determination, too. That there was a problem with his knees was obvious, but he was never heard to complain. It slowed him down but it didn't stop him.

Gradually the couple had become part of the community, bringing to it their own characters, individual and collective. Anna's culinary contributions to any gathering were always very welcome. Hearty but different to local traditional fare, even when she worked from a 'traditional' recipe her food bore her own distinctive touch. Edmund got involved in local events and activities, from the mundane like the chess club in Bergen, to the more unusual like the annual group plunge into icy water to mark the start of winter. The big man's choice of swimwear raised some eyebrows, as did his explanation of the term "budgie smugglers". But there was no doubting his enthusiasm.

He'd brought a new annual event too, introducing his neighbours to ANZAC Day. It was done out of particular respect for his grandfather and father, Arthur Senior and Junior, although there were generations of his family who'd served in a succession of wars. They'd been soldiers as well as cattlemen, he proudly told anyone who'd listen and some who didn't. Especially on April 25th.

"I think half of Bergen at least has heard about Arthur and Arthur," said his wife affectionately.

At first he'd stand at the bar in Bergen on that date, shouting drinks and telling his father's and grandfather's war stories. In latter years, with Anna's willing support, he'd started hosting a barbecue on their farm. Steaks, beer and rousing choruses of *Waltzing Matilda* and *I Come From A Land Down Under* in unlikely accents.

On hearing of this John B. wondered if he and Q could arrange to come back in a few months time. He was confident that this visit wouldn't last that long – his beloved was on a mission.

Watching the two women chat over their steaming mugs of wine Edmund was struck by a sudden flash of inspiration.

"There's been no snow today, so the road's not too bad. John B. and I have put chains on the Lemon's tyres anyway. Why don't you girls have a night out in town? We'll look after the kidlets, right mate?"

Stewart shrugged a little uncertainly, but said, "Sure."

He liked the idea on the ladies' behalf, he just wasn't entirely confident of

his own child-minding ability. Still, that was what their Dad was there for.
"Sure," he repeated.

Elizabeth and Anna looked at each other bright-eyed. The Australian nodded and smiled. The farmer's wife hadn't had a night out without husband or kids or both for what felt like a very long time.

"We-e-ell," she said, responsibility grappling with enthusiasm, "I guess if we're not too late home…"

Seeing their reactions John B. upped the ante. "If you know a nice place in town, spend the night. Saves you having to worry about the drive home. I'll shout the room, as a thank you for our board and lodging."

He knew he still had plenty of *kroner* in his wallet, and could always trust Q with his card to withdraw more. That suggestion took Edmund aback. "Um… yeah, that would work, I guess."

"Hey, come on old mate. You and I can fix breakfast for ourselves and these two little guys, can't we?"

"Daddy can burn water," said Ivy emphatically. Clearly something her mother had said had made an impression.

"Hey hang on, sprout! I'm not that bad! I can still fry up a pretty mean plate of fish fingers!" protested Edmund.

"Fish don't have fingers. They're called fish sticks," stated Little Don, who'd also clearly been listening to his mother.

The mother who now said, "And they are *not* having fish sticks for breakfast."

"If you've got bacon to go with that plentiful supply of eggs, I can make breakfast," offered John B. diplomatically. "Or point me at the oatmeal. My porridge won't be as good as yours, Anna, but it'll stick to the ribs."

Anna still looked dubious, although the idea was clearly tempting. Sitting in his preferred position on the floor the wizard threw an arm around Ivy's shoulders, and looked over to Little Don on the couch.

"What do you reckon? Does Mummy deserve a night out?" he asked.

"Yes!" they shouted in unison.

 The adults all laughed.

"That, my friends, seems a pretty ringing endorsement," said John B.

.o0o.

17 GIRLS NIGHT OUT

Before changing into a 'going out for the night' outfit that hadn't been worn in a while, Anna prepared a bowlful of pancake batter.

"Now, you *are* okay with this, aren't you?" she asked, handing John B. the appropriate pan.

"Yes Mum," he replied, tongue planted firmly in cheek.

"She's not your Mum, she's my Mum," said the ever-literal Little Don, standing just by the kitchen doorway.

"Alright. Yes, ma'am," corrected the guest cook. "Separate pan for the bacon. Ed knows where the maple syrup is, I'm sure."

Soon after, the ladies were dressed and ready to go. Anna was quietly relieved that the floral outfit she'd chosen still fitted – it really *had* been a while. In the warmth of the house she'd only draped her cream wool cardigan over her shoulders. Likewise Elizabeth, whose borrowed knitwear in an only slightly darker shade, was lying lightly on a teal top that she'd teamed with a longer skirt than she'd worn the day before. The Australian held a small bag that contained a change of clothes for the next morning.

"You look really nice, Mummy," said Ivy. "And so do you, Miss Elizabeth."

"I think so too!" added Little Don quickly.

The men were both smiling broadly, and it was John B. who said, "I reckon that makes it unanimous. Now ladies, go and have a good time!"

Hugs were given all round, and then they were off. Cardigans were in place for the chill night air between the farmhouse and the heated Volvo.

John B. trotted out to open and close the barn door and the gate. Sensitive to complaints that "they were cold just watching him", he'd thrown his spray jacket on over his t-shirt, although he did unzip it as he waved farewell while closing the gate.

Back in the house, Edmund had fired up the stove. He really wasn't as incompetent in the kitchen as his family made out, but he accepted their having fun at his expense with good grace. He loved the sound of his children's laughter.

When John B. came back into the kitchen he laid the first strips of bacon into their pan. He handed Edmund a pair of tongs and said, "Right mate, you're the bacon chef. I'll take care of the pancakes."

Despite the years of separation, the two men had settled easily back into comfortable communication that didn't require a lot of conversation. Watching from the doorway, the kids were impressed to see two people working together in the kitchen, saying almost nothing to each other, and producing something that smelled really yummy. Usually Mummy worked on her own, and if she did have assistance then the helper was working to a steady stream of directions.

All four were soon sitting down to satisfying serves of pancake stacks topped with crisp bacon and thoroughly doused in real Canadian maple syrup. An hour or two of cartoons on DVD followed, ostensibly for the kids' entertainment.

In fact, both men were fans of classic old Warner Brothers' animation. If asked, John B. would declare that Daffy Duck was his all-time favourite comedian. Wile E. Coyote was Edmund's slight preference. The children had their favourites too. The Road Runner for Little Don (possibly just to be contrary with his father's choice) and Pepe Le Pew for Ivy.

"She's going to grow up with a strange idea of romance," warned John B. quietly.

"Any bloke who wants to romance my girl is gonna have to go through me," replied his old friend.

The wizard put his finger to his lips and tilted his head in the direction of Ivy, sitting on the floor beside him. "Don't give her a challenge, mate. Remember what girls were like when we were teenagers."

Edmund laughed. "Why do you think I'm gonna be so tough?"

"Because you remember what *we* were like."

The kids had no idea why the adults suddenly laughed so loudly. Little Don looked around and gave an admonishing "Shushh!"

A few more cartoons (and mugs of hot chocolate) later, both children were yawning. They washed and went to bed without a murmur of complaint. Edmund read Little Don a short book about a monster in purple pyjamas, which the boy loved but barely made it to the end of before his eyelids slammed shut. In the next room, John B. read Ivy only a few pages about a lovable but trouble-prone dog before she too was fast asleep.

With a satisfied smile Edmund changed the DVD, selecting the top one off a pile of classic Westerns. At the farmer's direction John B. got a bottle of tequila and two glasses from the kitchen. The two men sat at either end of the couch with the bottle between them, and relaxed into *The Return Of The Magnificent Seven*.

They were soon joined by Marzipan. She jumped up onto John B.'s lap and gave a long studious stare into his eyes. There was a small *squeak*, apparently of approval. She then padded along the couch, stopping for a perfunctory sniff of the tequila bottle, before she climbed onto Edmund's lap, curled up and promptly went to sleep.

Whether John B. had quietly wished for it or not will forever remain a mystery, but that night Edmund and Anna's kids slept peacefully and com-pletely undisturbed by their father and his old mate, and the loud gunplay from the television that lasted into the early hours of the morning.

Meanwhile, having paid for a twin room at a convenient nearby hotel and dropped off their 'morning clothes', Elizabeth and Anna were dominating the jukebox at a rather fancy bar in uptown Bergen. Nobody was going to challenge them, although one hapless guy did try. He couldn't outstare or face down either of the women, far less both.

The barmaid was firmly on the side of the visitors – the only other females there, so the unhappy fellow really didn't have a chance. It gave his girlfriend a new perspective when he came home from the bar earlier than usual, soberer than usual, and with tail firmly between his legs.

The bar manager did at one stage of the evening have Words with the barmaid about her new friends. She in turn pointed out to him that it was good business to encourage having females at the bar. That was because wherever girls are, boys will follow.

The bar manager looked over and saw Elizabeth and Anna happily drinking wine with bourbon chasers (accommodating a favourite tipple of each of them). They were an undeniably attractive pair, and apparently not short of *kroner*. He decided that his barmaid might just have a point. And even if she didn't, he wasn't going to be silly enough to argue.

At one point the two new friends were comparing memories of high school dances. The good bits, the bad, the boys (several of whom fell into that latter category), the fashions and the music.

Elizabeth felt slightly at a disadvantage. Her mother Myrna had kept a tight rein on her social life, but she realised with hindsight that the curtailment and pressure to be "good" actually increased *after* she'd left school. It was as though Myrna had expected the teachers to provide a significant proportion of her daughter's discipline, and once their influence on the girl was done she'd stepped in to fill the breach.

There were still plenty of memories to share smiles and laughter about. A comparison of misheard song lyrics kept them both amused.

"They're called mondegreens, apparently," the Australian observed.

"I've heard the word. Wonder where it comes from?"

Elizabeth shook her head as she chuckled, "You might guess, but JB actually knows. He reckons it's from an old Scottish ballad – I mean really old, like the 1600s." Her voice took on a trace of the lilt she'd picked up during their stay on Islay as she recited, "Ye Highlands and ye Lowlands, oh where have ye been? They have slain the Earl of Moray, and laid him on the green. Only people thought it was, 'They've slain the Earl of Moray and Lady Mondegreen'. And somehow the word stuck."

"That's bizarre. That he knows that, I mean. Although, he and Ed did study history together didn't they? I studied some medieval history – it's one of the things Ed and I first discovered we had in common. Well remembered, madam, I'll have to try to file it away in my head, too."

"But there's so many of those lines!" laughed the brunette. "I was *sure* the Rolling Stones were singing 'I bet Jemima was a tinfoil queen'. I thought I was missing some slang code thing."

"Ah! I thought it was 'I betcha Mama wasn't yet fourteen' when I heard it," replied the blonde. "It was only when my best buddy actually bought the album and read the lyrics I found out it was 'I bet your mama was a tent show queen'. So much less interesting."

"And still a slang code anyway!"

It had been while they were still laughing at that thought that a man had come to the bar beside Elizabeth. Ignoring them both he'd ordered a large pilsner.

"Evening, mate!" said the Australian cheerfully. She was in an amiable mood.

"Eh? Ah – *guten abend, fraulein.*" The man raised his glass politely, but turned and walked away to sit at a table alone.

Elizabeth looked slightly put out, and said, "Hmph! I thought I might get a slightly warmer reaction than that!"

"You weren't flirting, were you?"

"No! Just being friendly. Wasted effort."

"Maybe he doesn't speak English."

"He knew enough to answer me, say 'good evening, miss'. I suppose at least he was polite enough to do that."

Anna looked over at the table and its lone occupant. She noted his sad gray eyes, their gaze moving slowly around the room without resting anywhere. He was a man clearly not at peace with the world.

The Florida native said to her friend, "Actually, he doesn't look very happy. Maybe he's here drowning some sorrows."

The brunette looked in the same direction, and admitted, "You're right. I guess you never know what's going on in other people's lives. Poor bugger."

The women would have been less inclined towards sympathy for Horst Bader if they'd known even some of the crimes that he'd been involved in. Certainly it was true that he did look unhappy. He usually did. If anything in life had brought him joy it had been a long time ago. Now he was just ruthless and efficient. If doing a job well brought him some professional pride, it didn't bring him any particular pleasure.

Deciding that the German speaking man's apparently pensive ruminations were none of their business, Elizabeth and Anna turned back to the bar and their earlier conversation.

"Does anyone really know the words to *Louie Louie*, do you think?" asked Anna.

"Not even the bloke who wrote it!"

They would have laughed less heartily if they'd known some of what lay behind Bader's gloomy expression – anything at all of what his employer had planned.

Later, back in their comfortable hotel room Anna caught sight of herself
in a mirror as she slipped off the dress she'd been wearing, and frowned
worriedly.

"Did I really look alright in this? I haven't worn it in such a long time.
With the farm, and the kids… well, I'm not the woman I was," she said
sadly.

"How do you mean?" asked Elizabeth cautiously.

"Oh, you know – time marches on. My skin doesn't glow like it used to,
my figure… well, I sag in places I didn't used to."

"Has Edmund said anything?" the Australian asked, remembering an
ex-husband who'd been very quick to criticize.

 Anna laughed. "Oh, he still says I'm beautiful! Silly man! I've told him
he's delusional."

That drew a thoughtful smile from her companion before she suggested,
"Why don't you try to see yourself through his eyes? Instead of trying to
make him see you through yours. If you're not happy with what you see,
is there a point to making someone else unhappy too? The danger is that if
you persist, one day he'll stop disagreeing with you."

 The farmer's wife was quiet as she considered that. Elizabeth, thinking
of her own history, recent and otherwise, waited a few moments before
speaking again.

"You used the word 'delusional'. A little while back someone said to me,
talking about what I see in John B., 'love is blind, I suppose'. He was actually there. I expected him to get angry or defensive or something, which
is what I was about to do – but he just shrugged and said, 'Not blind – it
just sees from a different place'. I like that."

 A broad smile creased the blonde's face. "So do I."

The shared moment of introspection further tempered the bond of friendship that had been already strengthened by the fun of the evening. Elizabeth lay on her bed, politely allowing Anna first use of the not-very-spacious bathroom.

"Do you really have to dash back to the farm first thing in the morning?" called the Australian.

"Well… I probably should," came the uncertain answer. "Why?"

"I just thought it'd be nice to have a little look at some shops while we're in town. JB would traipse around with me if I asked, but I thought it might be nice if you and I shared the experience."

Anna grinned into the mirror. It was another indulgence she hadn't allowed herself for a long time. "I think that's a great idea!" she announced.

With a broad smile of her own Elizabeth started typing a text to John B., letting him know they'd be a little later home tomorrow than planned. He and Edmund would cope, she was sure.

.oOo.

18 BONDING

John B.'s porridge might not have been quite up to Anna's standard, but there were no complaints, nor anything left in any of the bowls for Marzipan to surreptitiously lick clean. Certainly it was a breakfast that sustained a busy morning's work. The junior Mapletons may have been young, but they knew their jobs on the family farm and took great pride in showing off that fact to their Daddy's old friend.

For his part, Edmund was getting a new understanding of his wife's organizational skills. Thanks to her, the morning routine was by now so well established that even the cattle and chickens seemed to know where to be and what to do.

By nine o'clock the four were able to take a break in the kitchen over steaming mugs: coffee for the men, cocoa for the kids. The companionable domesticity had turned John B.'s thoughts towards the home life he'd left behind in Canberra. More to the point, perhaps, the renewal of an old and dear friendship had prompted him to consider the value of some other relationships.

Checking the time zones he found it was early evening in Canberra. With luck, young Darren would be home.

Darren James Bond shared the wizard's one bedroom cottage in the leafy suburb of Waramanga. When Stewart was in residence, the young man slept in something like a cave they'd constructed under the dining table. When he had the place to himself Darren moved into the bedroom, with John B.'s genial approval.

The younger brother of another of Stewart's old University colleagues, Darren had been an unexpected arrival in Canberra at around the same time as the incident that had apparently awoken John B.'s magical power, and remained one of the few who actually believed in those powers. An indulgent if slightly awkward acquaintanceship had deepened into a genuine close friendship, and while postcards were routinely sent it had been too many weeks since they actually spoke.

The phone in the cottage had been answered almost immediately, and both men were delighted to hear the other's voice. They chattered for some minutes, exchanging news. John B. decided against worrying his young friend by detailing the strange destruction of the *Warfish*, although he did make passing mention of "some weird stuff going on – nothing new there, eh?" which elicited a sympathetic chuckle. Darren had been closely involved in some of the wizard's perils.

Finally, after a pause Darren took a deep breath and said, "Listen, I know you don't do Facebook…"

"Give me time, mate. Q has got me joining the twentieth century."

"It's the twenty-first century."

"I know. I'm a work in progress."

Darren laughed. "Anyway," he continued, "I mean, in Facebook terms, I'm – ah – In A Relationship."

"Hey, that's great! Tell me more!"

The young man paused again, evidently nervous. "Goldie and I first met at the library, when you'd gone missing in Melbourne that time. Pointed me at where to find the help I needed. Then I called to say thank you, and we caught up again at a folk dance."

"Cool! Glad you're getting out a bit," responded John B. with a broad grin. "I did figure that having the whole place to yourself instead of living under the dining table might help your social life."

"It certainly hasn't hurt," Darren replied with a smile. The expression slipped a little as he said cautiously, "Um… I should tell you, Goldie's a guy."

There wasn't a moment of hesitation before John B.'s voice came through the phone. "Are you enjoying your life? Does he make you happy?"

"So far, yeah."

"Then that, my dear old friend, is all that matters. To me. To you. To Goldie I hope, and anyone else – well, their problem, not yours."

In Canberra, a nervous young man inhaled deeply and smiled. "Thanks mate."

"Hey, how could I wish you anything but happiness?" replied the wizard simply.

They spoke for a few minutes more, with Stewart explaining the delights of farming in the snow before Edmund signaled that it was time that they resumed some of those tasks. John B. had volunteered to help with a few maintenance jobs that Edmund's mobility issues made difficult. Not that he was a particularly skilled or experienced handyman, but with his old friend's supervision a few awkward little jobs could be taken care of.

Anna would be well pleased when she got home, and meanwhile she would admit to reveling in the opportunity to visit some of her favourite shops with Elizabeth.

In one small unpretentious boutique the expatriate American made a par-ticular point of introducing the owner Hannah Aldoy.

"This is the lovely lady who made our wedding outfits – mine, Edmund's, the whole party!" she enthused.

"That's an impressive effort," agreed the Australian, admiring the small range of clothes and material on display.

The seamstress bowed her head politely. She was a dark-eyed, dark-haired woman who looked to be of a similar age to both Elizabeth and Anna, less tall than either.

"There are some beautiful fabrics here," remarked Elizabeth. "Locally made?"

"Very much so," said Hannah with a smile. "I am a weaver by preference, a seamstress by financial necessity. There is little call for hand crafted sails these days."

"I can imagine!" laughed the brunette. "The motifs you use – they're based on traditional patterns, aren't they? I'm recognising Viking, Celtic… some Moroccan?"

"Moorish, perhaps," agreed the weaver. "You have a good eye."

As she continued to browse Elizabeth's eye was also caught by some of the small items of jewellery artfully displayed around the shop – each piece perfectly suited to the clothing it was near.

"Do you make these as well?" she asked Hannah.

"No, that is not where my talents lie," the woman replied with a pleasant, gracious smile. "These are designed and made in Tallinn, in Estonia. The silversmith is a very old friend of mine."

Anna was admiring a stylish tuxedo that she sadly knew her husband could never be convinced to wear. "Maybe we could find something nice for John B. as a 'thank you' for last night? Something in purple, I presume."

"He'd say there's no need for thanks, but it's a lovely idea. Oh! We've got some material we were given when we on Islay – a purple tartan. Hannah, could you do something creative with that?"

"I'm sure I can. I'll need measurements, of course," replied Hannah. "You can bring him in, or I could call in to the farm if that's easier for you."

After a moment's thought Elizabeth said, "That might be the best thing, if it's not too inconvenient for either of you. It'd give him less chance to wiggle out of being dressed in anything other than jeans and a purple t-shirt!"

Just for an instant a look of curiosity flashed across Hannah's face, unnoticed by the other two women. She consulted her appointments book and said, "Would Friday suit? Around lunchtime? I can get Astrid in to look after the store for the afternoon."

That was agreed to be mutually convenient, so the arrangement was confirmed.

Elizabeth did like the idea of a gift of her own for her beau. She indicated a pendant that had caught her eye.

"That stylized face, or mask," she said. "It looks African and Celtic and Maori all at once. I'll take that, please."

"An interesting choice," said Hannah as she slid the pendant onto a smooth leather cord. "It is based on an old Viking design, worn as a protective amulet when travelling."

The brunette smiled as she paid for the gift. "Sort of the Saint Christopher medal of its time, hey? Well, I don't believe John B.'s in need of any more protection than he already seems to have, but it's a lovely piece and I reckon he'll think so too."

Her cash register hid the curious expression that again momentarily clouded Hannah Aldoy's features. By the time she handed over Elizabeth's change, a pleasant shopkeeper's smile was all that showed.

As the two friends ambled back to where the Lemon had been parked they chatted about Elizabeth's proposed novel. A visit to the library was considered, but Anna wasn't sure how substantial the English language collection might be. But the bookshelves in the Mapleton abode did feature a few books on local and regional history that might be helpful, she averred.

"Look, why don't you stay on the farm for a week or three to really make a start on the book? Compile your notes properly and work on the actual story itself."

 Elizabeth was delighted at the offer, and impulsively accepted. It did seem an ideal environment from which to immerse herself in thoughts of a Viking past. Neither woman could imagine either of 'the boys' objecting.

Anna smiled enthusiastically at the prospect and said, "You'll find it a good place to work – I'll keep the kids out of your hair while you work, and otherwise it's completely peaceful."

.o0o.

19 BOARDING

On Wednesday night both John B. and Elizabeth accompanied Edmund into town for the regular meeting of the chess club. Neither could be described as an avid player, although both enjoyed the game. But it was a night out, and the farmer was keen to introduce them into a significant part of his social circle.

The visitors were mildly surprised at the number of members. There were more than forty boards set up in the hall, and even though they'd arrived early, many were already in use. The club's President, a snowy-haired gentleman named Harald Carlsson, and the secretary Ingrid Lofgren, greeted the visitors warmly.

Harald insisted on requesting the honour of a game against the "lervly young Oostralian lady". While Elizabeth struggled not to laugh impolitely at his accent, she was impressed by his manners and charm, so happily accepted the invitation.

Rather than play against each other, the two Australian men waited with the secretary to be pitted against whoever would arrive next. Inge reminded John B. of Scarlet Burke – a former work colleague and friend who'd faced death alongside him in the deserts of the Outback in his early days of wizarding.

The Norwegian woman's dark blonde hair was tied back in a too-severe bun, and her glasses seemed too big for her face, dominating what might otherwise have been quite pretty features. The three made amiable small talk for a little while, the secretary pointing around the room at club members who could be deemed interesting (if you used a broad enough definition of 'interesting').

It wasn't long before two more men arrived together – a striking blonde man in a black turtle-neck sweater and black pants, and his older companion smartly dressed in a grey suit. Edmund knew both of them, by sight at least although he'd not spoken at length with either. John B. thought he spotted an immediate tension about the younger of the two men when near his old friend and host, but chalked it up to perhaps a past defeat on the chessboard.

It was this man that Ingrid suggested might play against Stewart, and the local quickly agreed to the suggestion. That added further fuel to John B.'s suspicion of a recent loss.

Before going to their boards the diplomatic Ingrid made sure she introduced both of the new arrivals to the Australian visitor. John B.'s opponent was Eidur Johannesson, and his companion was introduced as Doctor Bischoff.

"Kevin," insisted the doctor as he held out his hand. As they shook hands both men stopped suddenly at their first touch, before continuing with strange caution. Both had felt something like a spark at the moment of contact. Static electricity?

The doctor seemed genial enough, but there was something vaguely familiar about him. As they stood facing each other John B. found himself looking at his own reflection in the doctor's mirrored sunglasses that he hadn't removed.

"An old poker player's gambit – unusual for a chess player," the wizard remarked.

"Pardon? Oh – my glasses. Ah, nothing so shrewd, Mr Stewart. I just find the bright lights in the hall somewhat uncomfortable," Bischoff explained.

He carried himself with an air of casual power. Brown wavy hair with a hint of silver around the temples, high cheekbones and fine features – suddenly John B. saw the resemblance. Bischoff's face reminded him of Q. Unconsciously he glanced over to the table where his beloved was competing with the club president.

Bischoff's eyes followed the glance, and the grey-suited man gave a momentary start. John B. was still watching his sweetheart so he missed the reaction, which had been swiftly suppressed.

"Enjoy your time with us, Mr Stewart. You will find my friend Eidur a most worthy opponent." With that, Bischoff strode away to the table Inge had indicated. Edmund shrugged and followed.

John B. made a similar gesture and accompanied his opponent to the table that Inge directed them to. If Kevin Bischoff had seemed familiar at a vague visceral level, Eidur Johannesson was familiar in quite a different way.

As they settled down on opposite sides of the board Stewart looked at the Norwegian, who seemed only to have eyes for the game. If the black clothing was his normal attire in a similar manner to the Australian's own purple, it had to be admitted that it suited him. He had an almost stereotypical Nordic look: blonde hair, smooth lightly olive skin and piercing blue eyes.

Abruptly the resemblance dawned on him. The face he'd seen briefly on the night that the *Sailors Rest* burned, on someone in a similarly coloured (if rather coarser) outfit.

"Have you spent any time on Shetland?" the wizard asked casually.

"Not since my childhood. Why do you ask?"

"Oh, you just… remind me of someone. No-one I know, just someone I saw briefly in my travels."

"Ah. I do not travel much. Your move."

All three Australians were soon engrossed in their respective games. Elizabeth chanced to be sitting with her back to the others' tables, so she was quite oblivious to the frequent glances that Kevin Bischoff cast in her direction. Undistracted, she was able to concentrate fully on what was soon a good battle of wits and tactics with the president. Harald had started out with an intention of playing graciously but swiftly realised that his opponent needed no favours to be an effective match for his experience. It was a good challenge for both of them.

Edmund and Kevin made some polite conversation as they played, with the doctor casually enquiring about the cattleman's guests. The news that the pair had arrived from Shetland doing some research into Elizabeth's family history provoked no outward reaction, but it was no coincidence that Bischoff's concentration was thereafter not its usual self. He had played and defeated Edmund before, although the farmer was no slouch at the game. Edmund naturally applied a very military strategy to his play – more likely a product of his early training than genetics, whatever he may say about his forebears. The older man normally played a long, strategic game, but tonight found himself being outfoxed by the expatriate Australian in ways he wouldn't usually fall for. Although his glasses hid the fact, he was spending more time watching the back of the brunette at the next table than watching his own game.

A few tables away John B. was having less success than his old friend. He hadn't played chess for quite some time, while his opponent was clearly a much-practiced hand. The Norwegian indicated a preference to control the black chessmen, to match his outfit perhaps, which Stewart was content to indulge. Eidur played much like his grey-suited mentor: a thoughtful, strategic game with moves and countermoves thought out well in advance. John B. was much more impulsive, playing on instinct and re-action. His unpredictability made him a tricky opponent for the measured, cautious man in black.

Losing one of his white knights to a spur-of-the-moment play, John B. was sanguine. With something like a laugh he said, "I'm afraid I don't have Edmund's tactical nous to challenge yours. I don't have his military background."

"Yes. I have heard of Mr Mapleton's upbringing. Repeatedly. All of us here have heard his stories, and been invited to his annual celebration of his family's part in the wars."

Something in the cold voice rankled with John B. "I don't reckon he quite sees it as a 'celebration' so much as a mark of respect. Not unreasonable to hold your family in high regard, surely? I admit, it's always struck me as a bit of a shame that it's the military elements of their history that seem to have been what the generations before Edmund valued. But he's making up for it with the whole 'proud tradition of cattlemen' thing."

"But he does not… *let go* of that military history either," observed Johannesson, an edge in his voice. "I find it… inappropriate."

"You're a pacifist, then?" asked John B., with some sympathy.

"No. But I do not think that the British forces and their Allies should be glorified on Norwegian soil."

 John B. pondered that remark over the next few moves. He wished Wilko was available for a quick consultation – military history was much more the Tasmanian's forte than his own. He mentally assembled such information as he could remember, at some cost to his concentration on the game.

 He'd lost two pieces by the time he said, "Norway was officially neutral, yes? Until the Germans invaded and occupied the country in 1940."

"The 'invasion' you speak of was not regarded as such by all Norwegians."

"Fair enough. There were people in Britain who thought they'd be better off under Hitler than Churchill. I don't doubt there were similar sentiments here. I know there were some actions taken against the Germans here, with some local support," Stewart suggested casually, thinking of the 'Shetland Bus'. "I'm not aware of the Allies targeting any Norwegian personnel, like happened with some of the French who threw their lot in with the Germans."

"When the British bombed the docks at Kaafjord in 1944 there were Norwegians killed and injured. The lie was told that there were 'no civilian casualties' but there are those of us who know otherwise!" The edge in Eidur's voice was noticeably sharper.

"Well, sport, it's your country, your local knowledge – there's an old saying that history is written by the survivors. A lot of times it's written by the victors. That doesn't mean that other stories aren't true."

"Mmph. There was a fishing boat destroyed at Kaafjord, with fourteen crew killed or injured. The 'story' was that this was an armed trawler operating in German service. A convenient excuse!"

Stewart momentarily scanned the face of his opponent, who was glaring down at the board. Clearly this was personal. "So, not true then? You know that?"

The only reply was a grunt as a rook was moved into a threatening position. John B. considered for a moment, and then moved one of his own rooks onto a square previously protected by the piece Eidur had just moved.

"Check, I think," said the wizard mildly.

The Norwegian flinched very slightly. He'd let his irritation – no, let's face it, his anger – distract him. He inhaled deeply, but quietly, through flared nostrils. With glacial calmness he said, "I must go to the lavatory."

John B. shrugged and smiled. "No worries. A man's gotta do what a man's gotta do."

Eidur gave a small nod of acknowledgement. Both men were playing a game of diplomatic courtesy, each to their own character. John B. looked over at his companions.

Each game appeared finely balanced. Harald retained a few more pieces than Elizabeth, but from his worried expression Stewart realised the President was not in a strong position. The board between Edmund and Doctor Bischoff had been stripped of a lot of pieces, from both sides. Both players were strategists, the doctor in particular willing to sacrifice pawns in the service of his powerful queen.

The wizard noticed that between moves Kevin's head was often tilted not toward his opponent, but in the direction of the Australian woman a few tables away. The mirrored glasses made his expression hard to read. Edmund didn't seem to mind the lack of conversation – it helped him to concentrate.

Johannesson returned from his 'comfort break'. As he crossed the room he stopped briefly to converse for a moment with his mentor. They spoke softly in Norwegian, so Edmund completely missed any of what they said.

Returning to his own table, the man in black inhaled deeply as he sat down.

"Feeling better?" asked his opponent politely.

"Thank you, yes," replied Eidur, who proceeded to prove it by extricating himself from 'check' and immediately going on the offensive. He'd evidently used the time of his break to map out a strategy. A few black pieces, mostly pawns, were sacrificed but there was an inexorable build-up of force that drove through John B.'s haphazard defence. Some advances were held off, but the end was not long in coming.

Stewart was casual about the loss, but gracious. He shook the Norwegian's hand and complimented him on his effective play. Eidur did not gloat, to his credit, but his manner indicated that he had always expected to win.

"You provided a challenge, Mr. Stewart," he said politely. It was impossible to tell from the even tone whether he enjoyed or resented being challenged.

The wizard grinned in response. "A bit of fun, eh? Thanks."

Neither of them was interested in starting a new game, either between themselves or with any of the handful of other members milling about after completing their games. Instead they stood at a discreet distance watching their companions' matches.

Perhaps Harald Carlsson's early underestimation of his opponent caught up with him, as Elizabeth checkmated him, trapping the Club President's king between a knight and her queen.

Carlsson laughed good-naturedly. "Vell played, madam!" he said heartily, and shook her hand.

The brunette smiled in return, and enjoyed the polite applause of the few spectators, as well as an enthusiastic hug from her beau.

"I always love just how powerful the queen is in this game," she remarked airily.

At the next table, Kevin Bischoff looked up sharply at that remark. Yet again his heard turned towards the pretty woman who sat with her back to him. He quickly turned back to his board as she went to stand up.

Under the gaze now of several club members, as well as the Australian visitors, the doctor focused his concentration. Even as distracted as he'd been, the man in grey proved too strong an opponent for Edmund. He finished with less pieces on the board, but now moved them with ruthless precision and forced the cattleman into a position where there was no choice but to concede the game.

"Whoa, you changed gears there!" said Edmund. "Well done."

Congratulations and polite thanks were exchanged. A casual observer would have been forgiven for not realising that Bischoff and Johannesson had won their games, though. They quickly withdrew from the company of the other members and exchanged a terse quiet conversation of their own. Neither looked happy, despite their victories.

If any of the Australians noticed, they gave no sign of it, mingling freely with other club members and accepting drinks. The chess club was not officially licensed, but a few people routinely brought 'refreshments' to share. Notable amongst these was a local vodka flavoured with berries from the hill country.

Eidur and his mentor offered quick, barely courteous farewells to the group as a whole before exiting. They would continue their own quiet conversation out in the darkness of the Bergen night. It was a conversation well suited to darkness.

.oOo.

20 A SHOT ON ICE

It was not an assignment that Harold Worcester was pleased to have taken. His business partner was little more enthusiastic, but they had to acknowledge that their employer was a prompt payer of their substantial accounts. It was prudent to stay on the right side of him.

Neither 'businessman' realised that Eidur Johannesson considered this would be one of the last, if not indeed the very final, job he would engage them for.

The conversation over the chessboard had brought home to the Norwegian just how much contempt he felt for Edmund Mapleton and his damnable 'family history'. The expatriate Australian was not worthy of the attentions of one of the great spirits he could now summon to do his bidding, but that history did place him on the great ledger that needed balancing in Eidur's mind. Twisted as that mind might be.

Johannesson had been more peremptory than usual in giving his directions. Had he been a little less dismissive in his tone and manner the two professionals might have been pleased that he gave them so much latitude in carrying out the assignment. He gave a who, when and where, and left the how up to their choice. And he had no interest in being present for the kill, unlike some previous occasions.

Now it was quite late on Friday morning. They had received their instructions on the previous morning, and made arrangements quickly. Their quarry was a farmer, known to carry out most of his chores across the morning. The two shooters had placed themselves in quiet areas of the property, figuring to catch their prey unawares as he was at the further extent of his rounds.

Although neither man had any remotely agricultural background, they knew enough to realise that those 'rounds' could not be predicted with

certainty, so settled themselves at different parts of the farm. Their van
was parked neatly between them, for ease of a quick departure. They were
unsure of how connected their conventional mobile technology might be,
so each carried a small device that would buzz at the press of its counterpart's single button. One buzz meant job done. Two meant that there was
a problem and help was required. Three buzzes – get the hell out.

The weather was turning. A storm, or perhaps just a serious fall of snow,
was not far away. Harold was sorely tempted to press three times, get to
the van ASAP, and leave this behind. He'd been crouched behind a tree
and low shrub overlooking a path for some time. The cold and discomfort
had him wondering, for the first time in his career, if he was getting too
old for this crap.

*

The chores around the farm had been completed with enthusiasm and
efficiency. The two visitors had learned quickly, and added much to the
speed with which things were accomplished. The 'must get around to'
maintenance jobs had been mostly caught up with so now the mornings
were 'business as usual'. After the usual early start, things were largely
complete by about ten. Adults and kids were back in the house, enjoying
mugs of their favourite warm draughts.

The 'kidlets' were in their respective rooms studying, with Edmund moving between them, gently guiding them through their maths problems.

Elizabeth stretched leisurely, looking forward to spending the rest of the
day writing.

"I think I might go for a stroll. Soak up the landscape," she said.

"Make sure you rug up. There's supposed to be a change coming through
later – I'd hate you to get caught out there without enough protection!"
called Anna from the kitchen.

The brunette pursed her lips in irritation. "My sweater and coat are still damp from last night and this morning. I have to admit, I don't fancy wearing them again…"

John B. looked up from a history book and shrugged helplessly. He knew his own light spray jacket would be quite inadequate for his beloved.

Anna stepped out of the kitchen and gestured towards the entrance vestibule and said, "You're welcome to borrow some of my stuff, or Edmund's. There's a parka there that ought to keep you warm."

"Thanks mate," said Q. "Sounds ideal. I just want to wander around for a while and immerse myself in the environment."

The cattleman's wife looked concerned. "Don't get caught out there if it turns nasty. Take Arthur's old greatcoat as well. And don't forget that Hannah's coming after lunch to fit the clotheshorse there for his new outfit."

"Yes, thank you," responded John B. drily.

"I won't forget, don't worry," said Elizabeth. "I'll be back in plenty of time to make sure he doesn't wriggle out of it!"

"Would I do that?" her beau replied with transparently false innocence.

He was quite content with his wardrobe of jeans and t-shirts, and while he genuinely appreciated Q's efforts to expand his apparel, the notion of being a "clotheshorse" was as natural to him as a badminton racquet would be to a jellyfish.

Laughing, Elizabeth donned the parka and draped the khaki greatcoat over her shoulder.

"See you soon," she called, waving as she walked out.

She set off on a stroll around the paths of the farm she'd quickly come to know well. There was a particular spot, out near the edge of the property, where the view was just what she had in mind as she contemplated the lives of her Viking ancestors.

She allowed herself a small shiver as a gust of wind blew around her legs. The dark wool leggings under her tweed skirt were good, but not that good. Fortunately Edmund's grandfather had been a tall young man, so his coat came well down over her calves. Buttoned up, it limited the length of her steps somewhat, but that was a small sacrifice worth making. It kept out the worst of the wind as she ambled along the path on the ridge. Spread out before her were paddocks of snow, spiked through with bare trees and fence posts. It was easy for her to roll back nine or ten centuries in her mind as she looked out and composed her story.

It was fortunate for Q that it was Worcester who shot her. He was slightly less skilled than his partner, whose trusty Luger would have had her dead before she fell. As it was, the impact of the bullet entering her back propelled her off the path into a snowdrift, and the shock of landing in the cold mass robbed her of consciousness.

The Englishman saw the bloodstain spreading across the back of the greatcoat. He didn't clamber down to turn over the body. He didn't realise that the face in the hooded parka under the coat wasn't that of the farmer he'd been commissioned to dispatch. It was an uncharacteristic error that was perhaps attributable to his resentment of the way he felt their employer was now treating him and Bader.

Hands shoved in his capacious pockets, Worcester turned and walked back the way he'd come. The little communication device was jabbed once. A single buzz – job done, let's go, he signalled.

Harold was muttering softly to himself as he headed for the van. As far as he was concerned, this job would be the last for someone who didn't respect the team's professionalism. That was ironic when in this instance his professionalism had let him down.

Not only had he shot the wrong target, but also the victim wasn't actually dead. Not yet, anyway.

She'd landed in the snow at such an angle that there was still a passage
of air for her to breath, although that breathing was shallow and getting
shallower. The cold of the snow was rapidly dropping her body temperature. It was soon down to 25 degrees – a dozen below her normal. That
was what was saving her. Her body functions slowed in the chill, preventing her from bleeding to death, and keeping organs such as her brain from
deteriorating.

Still, it wouldn't sustain her long.

It didn't need to.

.o0o.

21 COLD, STEEL

John B. had followed the same path. Mere minutes after his beloved had set off on her stroll, Hannah Aldoy had arrived at the front door.

Concerned at the prospect of deteriorating weather, the seamstress had decided to come to the farm early. It was the wizard who'd answered the door. Stewart had been his usual genially courteous self, but somewhat distracted by the book he'd been engrossed in, he wasn't quite aware of Hannah's reaction.

The weaver had taken his outstretched hand, but stared as though she'd found a diamond in a cheap box of chocolates. When there was no glint of recognition on the man's part she'd quickly composed herself, but there had been a note of puzzlement in her voice as she'd introduced herself.

Anna had emerged from the kitchen and introduced the two 'formally'. They were both polite, but unusually reserved. Hannah's attitude seemed deliberate, but now it was Stewart who was unaccountably puzzled.

Certainly the new arrival was physically of a type he'd often been attracted to – dark haired, not tall but buxom (the only characteristic that might perhaps have been expected of a stereotypical Scandinavian woman).

When he'd made a diplomatic remark to that effect Hannah replied, "I am not entirely local."

Her voice suggested that she'd thought that Stewart should have known that.

"I'm sorry – do I know you from somewhere?" he asked. "I thought from what Anna said that you'd been in business here for quite some time, and you look too young for me to know you from…"

"I'm older than I look. Some of us just are, yes?"

Puzzled at the evident awkwardness, Anna stepped in to defuse the moment by suggesting that while she gave Hannah the tartan fabric, John B. should go and fetch his beloved. He very hastily agreed, which was how he came to be trotting up the path along the ridge, following Q's tracks in the snow.

And how, when those tracks suddenly stopped, he found her body in the snowdrift scant minutes after she'd landed there.

Asked later how he'd kept his wits about him in those awful moments, John B. couldn't offer a cogent answer.

"Instinct got the better of panic," was the best he could offer, without expanding on where the instinct had come from.

Crouched low beside her, he'd reassured himself, or perhaps convinced himself, that she was still alive. He moved her gently onto her side in what paramedics call 'the recovery position' and cleared space in the snow for her impossibly shallow breathing. He set his own light jacket to keep the freshly falling flakes out of his darling's airway. Then he clambered back to the path and ran back to the farmhouse.

Ran. *Ran.* Something he'd rarely if ever done since school days. He flung open the door and rapidly explained that something had happened to Q. Blood on her back – found her in the snow – get help!

Drawn by his old friend's dramatic arrival, Edmund looked out at the deteriorating weather.

"God knows when, or even if we can get a doctor out here," he said worriedly.

The wizard looked back over his shoulder and nodded. His eyes closed in thought for the barest moment. "Can't leave her in the snow, but must keep her cold…"

"The egg room is very cold," said Ivy quietly, as she stood clutching her father's leg.

A single nod from John B. as he said, "Egg room, good. Clever girl –
thank you. Next… I don't know…"

"We know a healer." Hannah's voice was low and intense.

Instinctively all of the adults knew that 'we' did not include the Mapletons.

The wizard and the weaver stared into each other's eyes.

"Old Black Guy." Stewart was not asking, he was stating a fact.

Hannah shrugged as if the name was unfamiliar, but was obviously agreeing.

John B. turned to Edmund. "Can you make a Skype call on your laptop?"

"Um… sometimes. If the reception is good enough," the cattleman answered uncertainly.

"It will be," came the wizard's reply in a voice of absolute conviction.

He dashed into the bedroom, pulled his mobile phone from his bag, and
rapidly thumbed up his meagre Contacts list. He tossed the device to
Anna, whose hands weren't encumbered by frightened children.

"The name you want is 'Scarlet'. Call her, get her to find Guy. I'm willing to bet he won't be far away. Please."

With that, he was gone back out the front door. For a moment the Mapleton family exchanged looks of bafflement and fear, then Hannah stepped
forward.

"I think you must trust him," was all she said.

Soon after John B. Stewart had first discovered his weird powers he'd
travelled to Central Australia, where he'd met a mysterious Aboriginal

elder who answered to the apparent nickname of Old Black Guy. One of
the very few things that Stewart and his travelling companions had learned
about the weather-beaten old man was that he was a healer of extraordinary, perhaps miraculous, ability.

 Among those companions had been Charlotte O'Hara Burke, better
known as Scarlet. She hadn't returned to Canberra with her friends. Unexpectedly she'd stayed in Alice Springs, where she'd taken a job in the
local library and become the unlikely girlfriend of a local bike gang leader.

 When Scarlet's phone rang she was just sitting down to dinner with the
members of '*Murph's Mob*'. She wasn't actually a permanent resident of
the group house that was the gang's headquarters – she rented a neat little
one-bedroom unit of her own several blocks away. But she did spend a
considerable proportion of her non-working time at the rambling residence
in the company of Murph, the charismatic former speedway rider who led
the Mob.

 Delighted to see John B. Stewart's name appear on the Caller ID, Scarlet
immediately launched into a rapid-fire chatter that would have astonished
her former workmates in Canberra. She'd been known as bookish, ec-
centric, and painfully introverted. Adventures alongside the unorthodox
wizard had profoundly changed her.

 Suddenly she realised that the voice on the other end of the phone wasn't
that of her former travelling companion. It was a woman's voice, with a
strange, indeterminate accent.

"I am sorry," said Hannah. "You do not know me, but John B. has asked
me to call you urgently. There is a person near to you who we must speak
to right away. I believe you know him as Old Black Guy."

Scarlet stared at the phone. How could this woman possibly know that
Guy was sitting two places away from her at the same table? The old
bloke was a frequent visitor to the house, sharing Murph and the Mob's
fondness for vintage motorcycles, but he almost never stayed for a meal.
This evening though, he'd been lured by the prospect of a kangaroo and

eggplant casserole jointly concocted by Scarlet and Murph. Or perhaps he was just encouraging some of the younger members of the Mob to eat more adventurously.

Perplexed she handed the phone over. Guy's skin, like ancient black leather, creased in puzzlement and concern. "Yeah?" he said.

"Healer – it is Hannah, the weaver…"

"Hey! How you goin' girl? Where are you now? Still up north?"

"Yes. I am in Norway even as we speak…"

"Dat's cool," Guy interrupted with a grin at his own joke.
"Not now. The wizard has need of your skills."

The seamstress quickly explained the little that was yet known, and that John B. was presently moving the victim into a cold room. Guy looked up and confirmed with Murph that he had both a laptop computer close by and a Skype account he could use on it.

"Gotta have 'em for business," explained Murph. The Mob ran several business enterprises from their headquarters, all of them legal to the surprise of some government investigators who'd come calling.

Briskly the old man got people organized at both ends of the phone. While Scarlet and Murph got the computer ready in Alice Springs, Guy himself sat cross-legged on his chair with eyes closed, deep in concentration. On the other side of the world, in Norway, Edmund got out his own laptop computer and dialed up his Skype account. Just as John B. had predicted, the connection worked first time. The farmer shook his head in amazement. He'd be doing that a lot in very short order.

His wife had dashed out to the egg room, accompanied by her children who would *not* miss out on an opportunity to do something, anything, to help their new friends. It took little time for them to clear the top of one of Anna's worktables. Eggs and trays were stacked out of the way just in time for John B. to walk into the cold room, Q's icy body in his arms.

The kids watched wide-eyed as Stewart laid Elizabeth on the table. They lived on a farm and had seen birth and death before, but had never seen a human being so blue and still before. Wordlessly John B. and Anna set about removing the layers of Elizabeth's clothing as gently as possible to expose her back. They packed the clothes back around the victim, now lying face down, to support her and keep some insulation around her extremities.

Wiping away the blood revealed a hole that was almost obscenely neat, dark against the paleness of the frozen skin. The bullet had missed the heart, but had clearly torn a path somewhere that blood poured through in a substantial quantity.

Hannah and Edmund came into the egg room, the latter bearing his open laptop. On the screen was Old Black Guy, wearing a look of intense concentration.

His expression was belied by his cheerful tone as he said, "Hey dere, brudder – been a while."

"G'day Guy. Thanks for being there, mate."

"It's what we do, brudder. You know dat. Now, someone hold dat machine so I can see what's goin' on. Okay, John B., you put your fingers exac'ly where I tell ya, but don't press. Not yet. But I need ya to concentrate."

Ignoring any pain in his knees, Edmund stood like a derrick as he held and tilted the computer as required to give the best view half a planet away. John B. moved his fingertips delicately around the entry wound, trying to *think* into the tissues. He was vaguely aware of a gentle presence in his mind, as if Guy was looking over his shoulder from inside his head as well as via the computer link. None of the others spoke. Most of them barely breathed.

"Okay, dat'll do," snapped the elder suddenly. "Weaver, you got pins an'

needles dere, don't ya? We gonna need da finest ones ya got. John B.,
I'm gonna tell ya *exac'ly* where to stick 'em, right? An' you don't miss de
mark by even de tiniest bit, ok?"

 Hannah nodded and unrolled the 'housewife' she habitually carried – a
length of quilted fabric in which were stuck dozens of pins and needles of
different shapes and sizes. Cunningly sewn pockets in the fabric carried
other tools of her art.

"Acupuncture to heal a bullet wound?" asked Edmund incredulously from
behind the screen. "How the hell does that work?"

"Ain't nothin' can heal the body like the body itself. Just sometimes ya
gotta give it a bit of help. Give it a push an' steer things along, like –
y'know?"

 Guy had ordered "some sort o' alcohol" to be brought, and the area
around the wound was carefully swabbed with good quality tequila before
the acupuncture began.

 For long minutes John B. pushed slender steel needles into the icy skin of
the woman he loved, guided by a man oceans away. Some of the needles
were inserted close to the wound, others into points on Elizabeth's ribs,
neck, hand or even ankles. Very precise points, on energy lines that many
master acupuncturists wouldn't have recognised. Edmond stood resolute,
aware that Guy needed his view to be held as near to motionless as possible. Still there was no hint of movement or life from the brunette on the
table.

 Anna had fetched warm clothes to rug up her family, even though the children had been ushered to watch from outside the door of the cold room,
several curious chickens at their feet. The kids were tasked with keeping
any hens from wandering in to the 'operating room' for a closer look.

"How can she survive being so cold, for so long?" worried the farmer's
wife.

"Reckon dat's what's kept her alive," came the aged voice from the computer.

"Some hospital emergency rooms chill patients down to twenty below normal before they attempt CPR," observed John B., his voice seeming as distant as Guy's.

"Now de tough bit," warned the black man.

Little Don's eyes widened, mirroring the expression on his father's face. Hadn't *this* been tough?

But the bullet itself had to be removed. At Guy's direction, John B. placed two fingers on either side of the wound, carefully between the finest of needles. He applied pressure, on and off, through each finger in a complicated rhythm.

"Weaver, you standin' by wid a pair o' tweezers?" asked the healer from afar.

Hannah started. "Me? But I am not…"

"You know enough, like we all do. An' ya got a good steady hand."

Anna shook her head and strode into the egg room. "So have I, and Elizabeth is my friend. Give me those tweezers please, Hannah. Guy, tell me what to do."

For a moment the seamstress looked as though she was about to protest, but the determination in Anna's face and voice won her over. She handed the long implement to the American woman.

Under the rhythm of Stewart's gentle palpitations something was slowly rising up from Elizabeth's back, squeezed up by deep muscles he was manipulating. Light from the overhead bulb glinted off metal.

"Grab a hold o' dat. Don't pull, just hold, till it's most o' de way out. De muscles is weaker near de surface an' won't quite finish de job."

The bullet came out, far more gently than it had gone in. Another swab of tequila was delicately applied before John B. sealed the wound with a few stitches of fine cotton thread, and then set about the slow process of removing the needles. The sequence of their removal was important, as was the timing.

When seven needles remained, Stewart was instructed to stop.

"You done good, brudder. Now you can start getting' her warm. Move de girl somewhere comfortable, den get dem last needles out. Den jus' let her sleep – lotsa sleep. She'll come good I reckon, but it'll mebbe take a few days. You folks all done real well. T'anks. And Weaver, I gotta say…"

Whatever Old Black Guy had to say was lost in a crackle of static. White lines fizzed across the screen of Edmund's laptop and the Skype connection was lost. The satellite had moved from its miraculously convenient position.

No matter. The impromptu medical team knew what to do. Anna and Ivy dashed to the house to prepare Elizabeth's bed. Little Don stayed to help his father get the egg room back in order – a task that John B. insisted be done immediately. The wizard wanted normal routine to resume as quickly as possible for everyone. Stewart himself carefully lifted and carried his beloved. Hannah walked close beside him keeping the insulating clothes and a blanket tucked around their patient, covering all but the small area where seven steel needles glittered, even in the falling snow.

"I think we must talk," Hannah said softly.

"Yeah, I reckon so. But not right now. I've got other priorities."

"Of course, Wizard. There will be time later. There is always time."
 John B. gave no sign of noticing the name the seamstress had called him by. Perhaps he assumed that Q had told her some of his story when they'd met in town. But really his attention was entirely directed on the cold woman in his arms. Nothing else mattered at that moment.

With the last needles removed from her body, and settled in a comfortable bed in the warmth of the house, Elizabeth underwent a remarkable transformation. The blue tint faded from her skin, replaced by a pinkish glow. She lay on her front, her head turned to the side much as she'd fallen when shot, but steadily her back began to rise and fall as her breathing became deeper and more regular. She was still deeply asleep, but there was a faint movement of her lips, as though she was talking in a dream.

.o0o.

22 THE NEXT MOVES

Very soon after Elizabeth was settled in her bed, Hannah had slipped away quietly. She promised Anna that she'd keep in touch to check on their patient's progress.

The Mapletons did their best to get on with the routine of the farm. Maintaining that routine, and tending to their wounded friend, was a valuable distraction for Edmund and Anna. Both harboured deep concerns about the shooting. Had it been an accident? A stray bullet from a neighbouring property, chancing to find a one-in-a-million target? Or was it deliberate? If so, why? And who? And would they strike again? Were the children at risk?

The police were called, but there was absolutely no evidence for them to work from by the time they could arrive on Saturday. Nearly twenty-four hours of falling snow had obliterated any trace of where the shooter had been. There had been no threats, no known enemies, and no apparent motive. Perhaps it *was* an incredibly unfortunate accident. Such things had been known to happen. Bullets travelled a long way, and if someone had, say, missed a tin can on a fencepost on a property somewhere uphill…

Without much conviction, the policeman said he'd ask at the neighbouring farm. He'd also make enquiries of some regular 'sources', but in truth he didn't hold out much hope. They had so little to go on. Even the retrieved bullet was of a type so standard as to provide barely any useful information. Sympathy was the best he could offer.

The victim's friends insisted that there be no publicity of the incident. The Mapletons wanted no attention drawn to themselves or their farm, and John B. had a definite feeling that if there had been a deliberate attempt on Q's life, it would not be shrewd to let the would-be killer know they'd failed. Let them wonder at the silence. The police saw no reason to disagree.

A comfortable chair had been set beside the bed. John B. took up residence in that chair, seldom moving in the ensuing days. He read, dozed,
held his darling's hand and stroked her hair as she slept. In the brief times
she was awake he'd talk softly with her, and help feed her oatmeal, broth
and other warming, comforting food to help with healing.

Late on Saturday when Elizabeth emerged a little more lucid from the fog
of her recovery, he explained what had happened. He couldn't say much
about the actual shooting, except that it had happened. Elizabeth herself
could add nothing. She faintly recalled some impact on her back and falling towards the snowy ground.

It wasn't until Monday that a doctor got out to the farm. He examined
Elizabeth, said how impressed he was at the neatness of her 'home-made'
surgery. He carefully replaced the cotton stitches with surgical thread that
would dissolve in time, and announced that all he would recommend was
monitoring her blood pressure. She was recovering well, he said. Time
and rest were all that were required now. The same pronouncement that
Old Black Guy had made in a brief call to John B.'s phone from Scarlet's
mobile on Sunday.

On Monday evening Elizabeth pleaded with John B. to stop sleeping in
the chair, and join her in the bed. He protested that he didn't want to dis-
turb the rest that she needed.

"Babe, I'm already pretty damn disturbed, haven't you noticed? Please, I
really would sleep better tonight with you lying beside me."

There was no arguing with the look in those green eyes. After dinner,
for the first time in days Stewart lay alongside his beloved. Q snuggled
close to him and draped an arm across his body. They kissed, and she was
asleep in moments with a blissful smile on her face.

Exhausted as he was, John B. lay awake for a while. He was delighting in
Q's nearness and her touch. But his mind was also hard at work, conjuring
hypotheses of how this had happened and what was to be done. As tiredness overwhelmed him the thoughts became increasingly far-fetched as his
subconscious floundered in the darkness.

Just before he fell asleep he whispered, "I wish I knew who was responsible for this. I want them to pay…"

*

Q was recovering, not rapidly but steadily. Anna's good food helped, as did the care and comfort of both John B. and the whole Mapleton clan. Even Marzipan had taken to sitting on the bed and squeaking solicitously several times per day.

It was an opportunity for Elizabeth to get stuck into her writing. Awkwardly at times, as she could only lie on her side or perch on a stool as she recovered, still keeping pressure off her back. But she researched and wrote for longer and longer spells before tiredness overcame her. And at her insistence John B. reinserted himself into the activities around the farm.

Over lunch one day Edmund offered to teach John B. some fencing moves.

"I suppose you'd need that on a farm, even here, to keep the cattle in," observed Q.

The farmer laughed, replying, "No, not that sort of fencing – I mean the art of handling a sword. It's a bit of a hobby of mine."

"How did you come to that?" asked John B., intrigued.

"I don't know if you remember, a long time back in Brisbane, we were in a fight outside a bar. Well, I say 'we' but you did most of the work. I decided I wanted to find a way of defending myself. I did a few Wednesday night martial arts classes, but they weren't good on my knees. But there were fencing classes advertised as being on in the same hall on Thursday nights, so out of curiosity I went along. Loved it, stuck at it, won a few competitions, despite being a bit immobile, so now I teach it."

"Not much use for self defence unless you're in the habit of going about with a sword at your hip," remarked Elizabeth wryly.

163

"No, but it's fun," Edmund replied with a grin.

"So you'll teach me some moves?" asked Stewart.

"Sure. Not quite textbook. It's kind of my own technique I've developed, since I can't move about quite as nimbly as the pros."

"Hey, I'm not big on nimble either, so that'll suit me. Thanks mate."

The lessons were a valuable distraction for the wizard, who was still reluctant to stray far from the side of his recovering sweetheart.

Twelve days after the shooting Elizabeth declared that her beau should accompany Edmund to the chess club that evening.

"Babe, you're going to wind up with cabin fever. Go out and exercise your brain," she insisted.

Stewart was reluctant, but understood her reasoning. In truth, both he and Edmund were glad of the break.

Anna was happy to play 'nurse' to Elizabeth, aided and abetted by her two offspring before they went to their beds. The Australian woman was making small adventurous forays around the house, and was delighted to sit beside Ivy's bed reading a chapter of *"Blinky Bill"* – Edmund was determined that his kids would grow up knowing some classic Australian stories.

By far the great majority of occasions when Kevin Bischoff and Eidur Johannesson 'got together' were at the fortnightly chess club. Bischoff, whose doctorate had been in business studies, spent much of his time buying and selling or arranging other people's transactions. His black-garbed protégé was simply misanthropic by nature. While capable of polite diplomacy, he preferred his own company. He'd created the ideal environment for himself on Svalgsay.

This particular evening the two men had elected to play against each other, a not uncommon choice that allowed them time for quiet conversation.

It gave Eidur more opportunity to learn from his mentor. Not just about chess.

The two Australians made a nonchalant entry to the chess club, and were greeted cheerfully by Harald Carlsson. Eidur and Kevin immediately noticed their arrival. The younger man in particular was barely able to disguise his shock. His mentor had to grip the black sleeve firmly to keep the younger man from springing up from their table.

"I nearly wasn't here tonight," Edmund told the Club Secretary Ingrid as he hung up his coat and hat by the door. "Had a bit of a ruckus up on the farm."

Bischoff and Johannesson did not have to strain to hear. Their table wasn't far away, and even when he thought he was being quiet, Edmund's resonant voice carried like a foghorn on a still night. The words 'nearly wasn't here' – particularly *nearly* – held Eidur's attention.

Arriving to join in the greeting, President Harald naturally enquired after the "lervly young Oostralian lady" who'd been his opponent a fortnight earlier.

The cattleman explained that she was at the centre of the 'ruckus', having been shot. Unconvinced and unconvincing, he outlined the theory of it having been a fluke accident. It was a miracle Elizabeth had survived, he explained, without mentioning any details of the nature of that miracle.

Bischoff's reaction to Mapleton's arrival had been surprise and some puzzlement. Now however his demeanour changed. His cheeks coloured, and behind the mirrored glasses his green eyes flashed in a way that John B. Stewart would have found disturbingly familiar.

He knew who the young woman was. He had plans for her, and had nurtured those plans for a very long time although he hadn't expected her to wander into his life when she did. To have almost lost her to a minor pawn's incompetence was intolerable. But there was more at play, he real-ised. The farmer's mention of a miracle… Bischoff stared at the other

Australian. Young Johannesson had found him disturbing, although Eidur admittedly liked almost nobody. But his protégé had noted that the scruffy man in purple was more complex and, he suspected, dangerous than his casual façade. Purple… Could he be…?

Harald and Ingrid almost fluttered in their concern. Was there anything that they or the club could do? No, Edmund reassured them. Elizabeth was recovering well on the farm. A large slice of luck and some quick action had saved her, and yes, it seemed to have been a remarkable and terrible accident.

"The chances of such a thing happening – extraordinary!" said Ingrid breathlessly.

"It's not something that will happen again." Given John B.'s recent mental state there was a remarkable lack of emotion in his voice.

There was something deep and dark in its tone though. Bischoff caught it, and recognised danger. Not a direct challenge, that was surely not possible – he could not know the truth. But that voice did more than threaten retribution, it foresaw it as certain fact.

It was the Club Secretary who offered a game against the visiting Australian, an offer he graciously accepted.

"You better watch out, John B.," warned the smiling Edmund as he sat down to a game against the President. "She's a gun player. You're gonna need a bit of magic to beat her."

It was a flippant comment, unremarkable to almost anyone who might have heard it. Not to Kevin Bischoff though.

Eidur's concern was at his contractors' failure to eliminate Edmund Mapleton. That was an error that required redress.

"I will use the Spear," he hissed softly. "It will not fail where my human agents have. I had not thought him worthy, but he must not cheat destiny."

His mentor shook his head sharply and discreetly indicated the shaggy haired man facing Inge. "That man is your greatest enemy."

"I have no enemies," said Johannesson calmly. "Enemies are a consequence of taking sides, and you know that is not what I do."

"Alright, he is your greatest obstacle. He must be destroyed!"

Eidur looked surprised. He'd never seen his mentor betray such emotion. It was disconcerting. But Bischoff had never misled him.

"What about the other Australian? The intended…"

"He's of no consequence! What happened there was a mistake on the part of your pawns."

"Yes, and that should be addressed," admitted the master of Svalgsay.

"Indeed it should. Let us ponder awhile."

Their chess game continued quietly for some time. Both minds were humming with malevolent creativity, none of which was directed at the board between them. Every so often a few soft sentences were exchanged, inaudible at any table but their own.

Ingrid and John B. finished their game. As Edmund had warned, the Secretary was a very able player. The Australian would have struggled even at his best, and he was clearly nowhere near his best. The game was played in good spirit though, and John B. admitted that he felt much better for the mental and tactical exercise.

"And of course for the pleasure of your company," he told Ingrid gallantly.

She smiled at the courteous flattery, and suggested a small libation. She had brought a bottle of Gevrey-Chambertin, an excellent French red wine that would be ideal to warm the spirits before going out into a chilly night. John B. was delighted to accept. He was first and foremost a drinker of single malt whisky, but knew enough to appreciate one of the excellent products of the Beaune region. An expensive treat here in Norway, too, given the country's tax regime, he observed.

That earned a shrewd smile from Ingrid. "You know our rules here, then? Fortunately, I choose to take holidays in the Cote D'Or and Cote Du Rhone districts of France, and the luggage compartment of my Fiat is spacious. To your lady friend's recovery," said the Secretary sincerely as she raised the glass she'd just poured.

Stewart shared the toast, pleased to let gratitude and optimism replace the anguish and anger that had been gnawing at him for days. Temporarily at least, he said to himself. There would still be a reckoning with someone, somewhere.

Bischoff and Johannesson had apparently finished their game very suddenly. The older man appeared at the side of the Secretary.

"How happy you both look," he said, wearing a benign smile of his own.

Whatever thoughts and emotions were raging in his head, the businessman was able to slip on charm and diplomacy as easily as one of his impeccable suit coats.

"Madame Secretary, might I commemorate our guest's visit to the Club with a photograph of the two of you together? Of course, Mr. Stewart, we look forward to you joining us again – but who knows what the future holds, eh?"

Realising that his evening's opponent was enthused at the idea, John B. was too polite to refuse. After fastidiously picking a few long stray hairs (not all of them female, or Norwegian) from the woman's dark coat Kevin took pictures on both Ingrid's phone and his own, "just in case". No one noticed him slip the hairs into a pocket of his coat. He accepted a glass of the excellent red and sipped it approvingly.

Eidur stood some distance away and declined the invitation to join the little group. The smile he gave didn't reach his eyes. He looked like a man with a great deal on his mind.

 Having reached an honourable stalemate in their game, Edmund and Harald joined the impromptu gathering. They were accompanied by a couple of other club members, one of whom also contributed a bottle of wine to proceedings. It was less impressive than Ingrid's, but a welcome gesture nonetheless.

 Knowing he had to drive, Edmund allowed himself one drink. Diplomatically he lingered over it while his old friend savoured a second glass, but the weariness was plain on John B.'s face.

"Time we got you back to the farm, mate," said the cattleman, with a genial arm around purple-garbed shoulders.

 The thanks that Stewart offered the club members were sincere. He'd needed the night out more than he'd thought. Q had been right, he realised without surprise. What was surprising was that just as they were leaving, Eidur Johannesson hurriedly approached them.

"I understand your concerns," he said quietly. He handed John B. a very plain business card as he continued, "I suggest that you visit these men. They are investigators, normally very good at what they do, in my experience. They are often reluctant to take on new clients, but I have called and made an appointment for you at their office tomorrow afternoon."

 The wizard read the address on the card, and then looked into the Norwegian's eyes. There was nothing to be gleaned there.

"Thanks mate. That's… unexpected. Please don't think me rude if I ask why?"

"I have been thinking of our conversation of a fortnight ago. Given what has now happened, let us say that I am concerned at the impression that Norway may leave upon you."

.oOo.

23 PIECES COME TOGETHER

The following day was a busy one for Eidur Johannesson.

Conversation with his mentor had gone well into the night. He had arrived back on the island rather later than usual after a chess club meeting, mooring his small fast motor launch in the early hours of the morning. Even with the amount of experience he'd had, it was powerful testimony to his skill as a sailor that he could so capably navigate the treacherous waters around his home in the darkness.

Notwithstanding the twists and turns of the evening, and the tasks laid out before him, Eidur slept soundly. He could turn off any turmoil or 'chatter' in his mind as easily as flicking a light switch. Serene in his own organizational skills, he allowed himself the luxury of sleeping an hour later than usual to compensate for the late start to his slumber.

Once awake he simply got on with his tasks. He telephoned Horst Bader and announced that he and his partner would be receiving a visitor at 2:30 in the afternoon. The German was instructed that they were to arrange a subsequent meeting with this man, at their convenience, at or before which he was to be killed. This afternoon's visit had been arranged so that they could identify their quarry correctly, the Norwegian explained, and thus avoid another mistake.

"Mistake?" queried Bader. He was already annoyed by Johannesson's peremptory manner, and had been about to take umbrage at an affront to their professional pride.

His manner quickly changed though when it was explained in a flat voice that the wrong person had been shot during their previous assignment. There was no rancour or obvious criticism in the voice, just the dispassionate recounting of a simple fact. How the mistake had been made was not discussed. Neither was there any mention of correcting the error. If Bader found that surprising he didn't say so. This new task, however, seemed to imply that their business relationship was expected to continue as usual.

What Eidur had in mind was completely different.

After the conversation with the contractor, the next task was to download and print a copy of the photograph that Dr. Bischoff had sent him. Inge Lofgren's face was not in this picture, only a shaggy haired man in a purple t-shirt.

Then some time was spent reviewing old footage from the security cameras around the dome house. This wasn't an arduous task. Eidur knew exactly what he was looking for, and had a good memory of the date in question. There. Images of his two 'hired guns' on their only visit to Svalgsay. One was chosen and this too was printed.

From a cupboard he fetched a small bowl that had been carved from a single piece of obsidian and then polished to a high lustre. That work had been undertaken a few centuries earlier, but the item was still in pristine condition. The pieces were cleared from the chessboard at the eastern wall of the dome – he already knew how that game was going to end anyway – and the black bowl placed at the centre of the board.

It was a short job to scoop up a generous handful of freshly fallen snow from outside the dome, and place it into the bowl. There it would soon melt, providing the purest water that Eidur could hope for.

From the same cupboard that had held the bowl came a square pewter box, no bigger than a cigarette packet. It held ordinary cooking salt, or rather, what had previously been ordinary cooking salt. Months earlier the man in black had drawn strange symbols in the surface of the grains with his fingernail while reciting a very old incantation. The salt, he knew, had become a powerful tool. Once the snow in the bowl had completely melted he would add to it a pinch of the transformed salt. With the right spell, the water would become a window through which he could briefly see through the eyes of another person.

On the board beside the bowl Eidur placed the strands of long hair that Kevin Bischoff had slipped to him. Rubbing them between his palms he'd rolled them into a small ball, which he weighted down with the pewter box so it couldn't inconveniently blow away before he could drop it into the water.

Satisfied with those preparations, he placed the two photographs together on the inlaid table at the centre of the room.

Content, the master of Svalgsay made himself a light lunch and then sat down at the western chessboard to muse on strategy.

*

Up at the Mapleton farm the routine chores had been completed in good time. The two Australian guests had now started to take an active role in the kids' home schooling, offering some variety that was welcomed by all four of the clan.

John B. provided quirky history lessons that were as entertaining as they were accurate. While the children laughed and made appropriate "Eee-ww!" noises at his descriptions of how Hippocrates sometimes made diagnoses by 'taste testing' his patients' wee (and other things), they would definitely remember the name of the 'father of medicine'. In years to come they would come to understand more of his significance, although Elizabeth's rapid recovery was already impressing upon them the importance of the science of healing.

Q was steadily getting stronger, and after the wizard's lesson she taught some arithmetic. She was pleased to find that Edmund had already given the kids a solid grounding in the study, and built on his example. She kept her lessons practical so Ivy and Little Don got a grasp of how and why arithmetic mattered: running a farm, planning an activity, managing pocket money. She couldn't make maths fun, but at least it could be interesting.

Although he couldn't shake a nagging distrust of Eidur Johannesson, John

172

B. decided to follow up on the card he'd been given. He'd drawn a blank on clues as to his beloved's assailant, both in terms of physical traces or any inspirations as to motive. As he climbed into the driver's seat of the Lemon, which Edmund was loaning him for the rest of the day, he patted the business card in his jeans pocket.

"I wish these blokes will lead me to whoever's responsible for shooting Q," he said grimly.

The cheery wave he gave the little group gathered at the farmhouse door belied the anger still simmering inside him. Edmund and Elizabeth in particular had their own strong suspicions about the wizard's state of mind – both of them had seen him fight before, and knew he could be both dangerous and reckless.

There was still some ice on the road, so John B. was suitably cautious as he drove into Bergen. Ahead of schedule for his appointment, his first stop was at the dock where they'd berthed the *Fior Ghaol*. He boarded the little boat and collected together some fresh clothes, mostly for Q, with an additional couple of t-shirts for himself.

As he walked back along the waterfront towards where he'd parked the car he happened to notice the name painted on a fishing boat moored nearby. *Svalgsay*. He'd heard that before, or seen it. Ah yes, marked on a map. It was the little island near where Miskwa Burns had come to grief. If he'd ever noticed the boat whilst in the Shetlands it hadn't made an impression on his memory.

It was a short drive to the other side of town to the unprepossessing building that was his destination. The business premises were as low-key and discreet as the business card. 'Well, that's a good sign of their professionalism – more substance than style,' he thought as he climbed the stairs to the first-floor office.

His knock on the door was answered by a cultured English voice that invited him to enter.

The room immediately reminded Stewart of Sam Spade's office in *The Maltese Falcon*. Perhaps tidier. The furnishings were more functional than decorative, and the walls were plain, a buff paint above timber panelling. There were two desks, set at right angles, and a pair of wooden visitors' chairs in the middle of the room.

Behind the desk facing the door sat the tall pale figure of Harold Worcester. His long fingers were interlaced in front of him on the desktop.

"Mr. Stewart, I presume?" he asked, his dark eyes not wavering from the purple-shirted man who'd just come in.

"Correct. I'm guessing by the accent you're Harold Worcester. You don't sound Germanic enough to be a Horst Bader."

"Shrewdly observed, sir," said Worcester with a small smile. He gestured to his left and introduced his business partner.

Getting down to business, John B. explained the circumstances that had brought him to the two men. Johannesson had given them no indication of why the Australian would be at their office. If so, their reception would have been very different, and their visitor would probably have been shot as soon as he stepped through the door.

Instead, the two business partners listened, neither of their faces betraying anything more than polite attention. Bader's eyes didn't meet those of John B., but the wizard noticed that the German's gaze didn't rest anywhere for more than a moment.

Worcester gave their visitor a practiced look of concern and said, "With so little to work with, I am unsure that we will be able to assist you, Mr. Stewart. But I will ask – if we *were* able to aid in your enquiries, what would you propose as a next step? Our sources and methods are not always aligned with those that the local police find appropriate to act upon."

It took scarcely a moment for the reply to be determined. "I reckon it's a matter I'd take care of myself."

"Dat might be – challenging," observed Bader, his voice neutral.

"I'm good with challenges, when they're important."

"Mm. Sir, I rather think you might be. Tea?"

Worcester stood, not waiting for a reply, keeping his back to Stewart and masking his partner's face as they exchanged looks. They didn't trust Johannesson, and suddenly wondered if the Norwegian was setting them up in some way. There was something innately dangerous about this man. Did Eidur think he was capable of being a threat to them? Had he been sent here to dispose of them, as they were to dispose of him?

"Thanks. Earl Grey if you've got it please," John B. answered casually.

As he reached the door of the little kitchenette the Englishman turned and asked, "How well do you know Mr. Johannesson?"

"Barely at all. Played chess against him once. Lost. That time."

As the Australian watched the tall man with whom he was conversing, Horst Bader silently slid open a drawer of his desk. He laid his hand gently on the Luger in the drawer, waiting to be sure his quarry was completely distracted. He neither liked nor trusted Johannesson, but would do this job as a professional. Then, once paid, he might just deal with Eidur himself.

Worcester spoke as he measured fragrant Earl Grey into a porcelain pot. "I think that you would do well to seek your answers on Svalgsay, sir."

The tall Englishman ignited the small gas ring under the kettle. Ignited it at exactly the same moment as a chant was completed on an island, miles away.

The master of Svalgsay had seen, in his obsidian bowl, that his three intended victims were together as he'd arranged. He couldn't hear them, but that was of no importance. He'd turned from the image in the water, taken up the ancient staff, and begun the incantation that would summon up Surtur, the fire demon, to do his bidding.

Several things happened almost at once in the upstairs office. Horst Bader drew his gun from the desk drawer, about to shoot. Unlike his partner, he would *not* miss. Instinct, or something like it, alerted John B. and he threw himself from the chair to the floor, rolling out of Bader's immediate line of sight. A massive fireball erupted in the kitchenette, flames belching out the doorway of the little room even as the walls shattered in the impact. The German's eyes flew wide – there was something almost… *humanoid* about what he glimpsed, as if a giant figure was crouched in the small space, a figure all aflame. Could *that* be Harold? Distorted in the glare of the sudden blaze? No. Harold Worcester died in an instant, turned to ash in a second at the centre of the incredible inferno. Then the figure was gone, and there was only fire, roaring at the timbers of the building.

Potent as Johannesson's magic was, it could only hold an entity as ancient and powerful as Surtur for an instant. But that was surely enough.

The worst of the initial explosion of fire passed over John B. Stewart as he lay on the floor, wondering what the hell had happened. Bader had dived behind his desk, dropping the gun as his sleeve caught alight. The old timber walls and fittings caught like matchwood. The two men would be trapped in moments. Men of lesser talents would perhaps be dead already.

Horst Bader dived through a window onto a fire escape, and put that rickety structure to the use it was intended for even as its metal groaned and started to pull away from the burning wall. Stewart stayed at floor level, moving for the door he'd entered by like a startled viper. He was out of the office and on his way down the stairs as the flames took hold of the floorboards.

Stewart was able to lose himself quickly in the crowd that was already gathering. He shook his head, trying to grasp what had just happened. The din of alarm bells didn't help his thought process. A small silver sedan went by at speed, apparently from a side street adjoining the burning building. The panicking driver was Horst Bader.

 The Australian wasn't in the grip of panic, but he wasn't big on reasoning, either. When he saw Bader fleeing, he just had to pursue. He pushed through the bystanders to where he'd parked the Volvo, and took off after the German.

 The driver of the little silver car had two advantages. A head start, and knowing where he was going. It was a matter of luck, or the coincidence that Wilko believed dogged his old friend, that the yellow Volvo followed the same route as Bader's sedan and finished up at the same location: the car park of Bergen airport.

 Further behind than he'd have liked, Stewart didn't actually see the German run into the terminal building. He spotted what he thought was the correct silver sedan in the car park, and pulled the Lemon into a convenient vacant space nearby. He checked the bonnet of the little car – the engine was still hot. That was a good sign. He didn't quite run to the terminal building, but he crossed the car park in long rapid strides. In truth, the Australian had no idea what he'd do when he caught up with the man. That would work itself out, he figured. The strategy of the 'long game' wasn't a feature of his chess playing, either.

 Entering through the glass doors he looked around. The terminal was quite crowded. A flight had just arrived and another would be departing soon, so there was a mix of travellers and their families bustling around the building, some of them running. Stewart thought he recognised one running figure, though, and headed after him.

 It was the wrong man, but his path took him near enough for the German to spot the distinctive purple t-shirt. Still in panic after the fireball in his office, the former East German security officer spun on his toes and shoved people aside. There was the escalator – the airline desks were upstairs and he had enough in his wallet to get on the first flight to anywhere that wasn't here.

Frantically he started to push his way up the long mechanical stairway, cursing that it didn't move fast enough to suit his needs.

A tourist had ignored the prominent "No Luggage" signs on the escalator going up – language was no excuse as the pictures made it abundantly clear. Near the top he lost his grip on his overweight suitcase. The heavily loaded luggage started to slide down rapidly.

Looking over his shoulder to see how close Stewart was, Bader had no chance to dodge. He looked up just in time to check his stride but he had nowhere to go. Thirty-five kilograms of toughened poly-carbide suitcase caught him amidships.

Suitcase and security chief plummeted together toward the bottom of the escalator.

The first thing Bader hit was his tailbone, causing him to bellow, *"Ach! Mein Arsch!"*

They were the last words he said, as the next thing he hit was the back of his head, just above the neck, on the edge of one of the escalator's steel stairs. He was dead by the time the suitcase came to rest on him at the bottom of the escalator.

The tourist stood at the top of the flight, looking embarrassed.

John B. couldn't help but see the commotion and crossed the forecourt, stopping quietly beside the small crowd already gathering around Bader. He knew immediately he'd get no further information from the man.

Slowly scratching his chin, he pondered what to do next. Worcester's final words played again in his mind. "Seek your answers on Svalgsay." The island? Or perhaps the boat?

The fishing boat was closer. He'd start there and continue on wherever, however proved necessary to find who was responsible for shooting his beloved.

.o0o.

24 TWO OF A KIND

On the island in question, Eidur Johannesson was tidying away his arcane 'tools of trade'. He'd wiped the little pile of black ash from the top of the inlaid table, not realising that it was the debris of only one photograph. When the picture of the two contractors had combusted in a bright flash, he'd been momentarily blinded and hadn't seen the other snapshot blown off the table by the little blast. It lay face down on the floor, half hidden by a chair.

Meanwhile, the man in that picture was driving the yellow wagon back to the dock where he'd seen the fishing vessel moored.

Svalgsay. 'The Swallower'. Could there be a link between the boat and the place he'd noticed on the map, or was it a coincidence? The name presumably had some local history, he reasoned.

Cautiously he approached the small vessel. No sign of life. The crew could be anywhere, though he suspected a search of neighbouring bars might locate some of them. He decided to brazen it out. Creeping around would only look suspicious anyway, so John B. strolled casually to the side of the boat, and climbed aboard.

The smell of the most recent catch, and many before it, assaulted his nose as he crossed the wooden deck. Looking like a potential customer Stewart poked around the deck, examining equipment. He had no idea what he was looking for, but was confident he'd know when he found it.

Whatever 'it' was, he decided to look for it below decks. Trying to balance caution with looking casual the wizard stepped down into the boat's small living quarters. The door was unlocked. Clearly the captain of the *Svalgsay* felt secure in Bergen. Good.

The captain's own quarters were small and quite austere. Nautical maps were rolled up and stored on a small desk, alongside a couple of hard-bound books. On a wall hung two photographs. One was a fading sepia snapshot of an older man, dressed in heavy fishing gear, with an attractive younger woman standing shoulder to shoulder with him. They were clearly close, but there seemed no obvious affection between them.

It was the other picture that caught Stewart's attention. It was a studio portrait, clearly much more recent than the sepia print.

The photograph showed twins in their late teens or early twenties. They were near enough to identical except for the gender betrayed by their hairstyles – his sculpted into a gravity-defying quiff, hers swept up in a bun with a protruding short tuft, like a pomegranate perched atop her head.

That hair was a light brown blonde, like a chardonnay that had spent a long time on oak. They were clear of skin and there was nothing but cold in their grey eyes. Both of them had full lips that might have been called sensuous in a face that showed more warmth.

Their expressions displayed something between indifference and contempt for the photographer. It was hard to imagine what might make either of them smile – only that it would be something that other people would find at the very least unpleasant.

The two young people in the photo were the very image of Hitler's Aryan dream. That was ironic since the fuehrer so little resembled the picture himself. Perhaps it was only natural that they embrace some Nazi philosophy.

John B. stared at the photograph on the wall. The hair was different, but he recognised the face. Faces. If they weren't side by side you wouldn't have known one from the other, especially if framed by a balaclava.

He was so absorbed in staring at the two faces he didn't hear the soft footfall behind him. A heavy rubberized flashlight hit the back of his skull, and the wizard was unconscious before he hit the floor.

On a farm behind Bergen, a green-eyed brunette looked up suddenly from the story she was reading two children. The faces of Ivy and Little Don reflected the puzzlement then concern that crossed her face. Even Marzipan, curled up on the reader's lap, gave a startled squeak. After a moment Q smiled a tight smile.

"You'll be fine, babe. I know you will," she said softly, then continued reading.

It wasn't long before the man in her thoughts woke – just long enough for him to have been tied to a chair in the wheelhouse of the fishing boat. A boat that had been cast off and was now at sea.

As consciousness oozed back into his head John B. opened his eyes slowly, trying to get some sense of his situation. Without realising it he groaned softly. The sound was just loud enough for the captain to realise that the prisoner was awake.

"Ah, good afternoon."

"Good afternoon, Captain," replied the captive. "I presume you're the boss."

The barest hint of a smile flickered across the young woman's face as she nodded while the wizard continued.

"I'd say 'nice to meet you', but I reckon we've met. Briefly, in Shetland. Funny thing, when I met Eidur at the chess club I thought I recognised him. Then he said he'd never been to Shetland. I had no reason to doubt him, so I just chalked it up to a Scandinavian 'look' sort of thing. Turns out I wasn't far wrong, eh?"

"Eidur is my brother. I am Inge. You are the Australian he has told me of, yes? He showed me your photograph the last time I visited him on his island."

"Island? Ah – right." The penny dropped for John B. "When the Englishman told me to 'seek my answers on Svalgsay' I did wonder. I'd seen the boat, and thought the name must be a coincidence. But it's not, is it? This boat was named for the island your brother lives on."

"The island that we both own," Inge corrected. "It is where we are now headed. I'm not entirely clear about why my brother wants you dead. I have no such particular desire though, despite your trespassing on my vessel. As I understand it, you are not the type of person we would normally be concerned with."

"I wish I knew what you were talking about. Type of person? Concerned?" Stewart's voice was mild, but he was confident his words would have an effect.

 Again the merest shadow of a smile crossed Inge's face. "It will do no harm to explain. Eidur wants you dead, he will make it so. His methods are – *different* to my own, but nonetheless effective."

 The skipper flicked a switch to activate an automated steering device, and turned in her seat to face John B. properly as she explained.

"Our parents amassed a considerable fortune over their lives, importing and exporting a great variety of inconsequential items. The business occupied the great majority of their time and attention."

"I see. Parental wealth, maybe even indulgence, but not much parental affection, eh?" Stewart kept his voice neutral, betraying no sympathy, condescension or sarcasm.

"I suppose not," Inge replied, equally toneless. "My brother and I had each other. Their passing was not mourned. Even before their deaths, we were mostly raised by our two grandparents, both of whom were more – *efficient* than kindly."

"Only two? Not a complete set, then. Whose –"

"One of each," Inge interrupted. "Father's mother, mother's father. Both were widowed during the Second World War."

This time there was a genuine note of sympathy in John B.'s voice as he said, "That's tough. And probably explains some of Eidur's sensitivity about the War. He was particularly toey about a fishing boat that was destroyed."

Inge looked puzzled. "Toe-ee? A strange expression. But yes, the bombing raid on the Tirpitz was responsible for the death of both of my grandparents. Oh they survived the raid itself. My father's father died from wounds treated inadequately, leaving his wife to raise their only son alone. My other grandmother was thought to have been too near an explosion. She seemed physically unharmed, but she lost her hearing and her mind. It took some years, but she wasted away, sitting in a chair staring at books while my grandfather tried to raise their three children on a fisherman's income."

"I'm sorry. I can understand the resentment against the British…"

"It is not resentment." Inge's voice did not rise, nor did her expression change. Her face could have been a carving. "Over ten thousand Norwegians were killed during that conflict, either in war or imprisonment – yes, many by the Nazis but that wouldn't have happened had Norway sided with Germany. That 'neutrality' was a mistake. It created an imbalance that needs correcting. This is the task that we have taken upon ourselves."

John B. took a moment to compose his thoughts. He wasn't sure if this woman's emotions actually could be inflamed, but this wasn't the time to find out.

More calmly than he felt he asked, "By killing ten thousand people from the British side? More than half a century later?"

"What are fifty years across all of time? Balance is ultimate, and eternal. We are instruments of that balance. For myself, I don't aspire to such a grand total of lives. I am content to do my own small part by dispatching those who have fought for the Allied forces, and those who idealize their memory."

Suddenly Stewart had a mental image of Edmund Mapleton leaning on a bar, waxing lyrical about his forebears and making an Event out of every ANZAC Day. And an image of his beloved Q, walking out of the house in an old, treasured Army greatcoat.

Perhaps Inge read the look on his face, or perhaps in some way she read something of his mind. "Had Eidur asked me to eliminate the farmer, there would have been no mistake. He knows I am reluctant to shed blood on Norwegian soil. His employees are normally efficient, but they are just that – employees. They lack our commitment."

John B. said nothing. Awkwardly, he turned in his chair and stared out the wheelhouse window, determined to keep a lid on his rage.

Unperturbed, the captain turned back to the wheel. The autohelm was useful, but she did prefer the feeling of control in her own hands.

Over on the island of Svalgsay, Eidur had just walked over to his obsidian bowl. He'd been in no particular hurry to clean it away. Now as he reached for it he stopped, struck by a moment of intellectual curiosity. What would it be like to see through the eyes of a dead man? Only blackness? Or might his magic be strong enough to pierce the veil and glimpse what lay beyond?

He passed a hand over the bowl and spoke the incantation. The water rippled, and an image appeared. The ocean. Waves. Part of a window frame. By the movement, it was evident that he was on a boat. The view faded, but Eidur had seen enough.

Somehow the Australian lived. The man in black crossed to the inlaid table and walked around it, staring. From the corner of his eye he glimpsed a corner of white paper on the floor, under a chair. Picking it up he realised that yes, it was the photograph of Stewart, barely singed.

With a deep inhalation of breath he laid the picture back on the table and went to fetch the Odinspear. Hevring the Riser would do his bidding, as before. She would not fail him.

Aboard the *Svalgsay* John B. had been mulling over what he'd learned. He turned back towards the homicidal skipper.

"You said *you* didn't aspire to killing ten thousand. What about your brother? Is he more ambitious?"

"Mm. That's a good word for it, yes."

"That's a lot of people. Any idea how he plans to manage it? I'm just curious. He didn't strike me as the mad bomber type."

"There is nothing about Eidur that is mad." Inge didn't turn to look at her prisoner. They were nearly at their destination and she had to keep her eye on the tricky waters. But she didn't need to look at him to speak, and praise the brother she so loved.

"Eider has always sought knowledge, where I have craved action. It was he who pored over the old books – the books that the grandmother we never knew died staring into. Ancient, powerful books."

For a moment John B. thought of Scarlet Burke in far-off Alice Springs. This sounded like the sort of reading matter she'd appreciate.

Inge went on with the ringing endorsement of her brother. "He has obtained the most powerful weapon in the world. Far more powerful than any bomb – any *modern* weapon. He wields the Odinspear."

"Hitler's Spear of Destiny? Sure it's the real one? There have been a few fakes over the centuries since the crucifixion…"

"No!" The snap in Inge's voice was the first hint of anger, fired by John B.'s casual dismissal of her brother's powers of perception and research skills. "This is the weapon of the All-Father himself. As old as this land, as old as the world. With it, and the knowledge he possesses, Eidur can command the Great Beasts of the past to do his bidding. They will be his instruments of destruction, the tools of our restoration of…"

Whatever Inge had visions of restoring, John B. would never know. Neither of them had been looking behind to notice the ocean's sudden strange behaviour. That was the moment when a great fist of water smashed down on the *Svalgsay*. Like the *Warfish* before her, the fishing boat was shattered, the wheelhouse slammed into the depths.

.oOo.

25 THE CLOSING GAMBIT

Just as had happened with Hevring's last attack, with the destruction of the boat the sea abruptly became calm. Debris was scattered across the surface of the water. Smashed timbers, fishing nets, pieces of equipment, bobbing in tangled masses like tiny islands.

Amongst the flotsam were two bodies. Both were face up, but only one was breathing. It was the one wearing a purple t-shirt. The body dressed in black was lifeless.

A small wave lapped over John B.'s face, dumping water in his mouth. Choking, he snapped back to consciousness, flailing arms and legs for a moment as he vomited brine. The wooden chair he'd been tied to had smashed under the impact of the Riser, like the rest of the *Svalgsay*, and now the restraining ropes were floating free of his wrists and ankles.

The wizard bobbed like a cork for some moments. His brain spun and his stomach still churned. Dimly he realised he was being carried by the current towards rocks – rocks that rose up from the sea like great predatory teeth. He grabbed a floating plank, grateful for the extra buoyancy. It wasn't a fast-flowing current, he realised as his head cleared. He relaxed into it, content to drift toward the shore until he reached a point where he could swim to somewhere he could climb out of the water.

Inside the dome at the centre of the island, Eidur stared at the surface of his inlaid table. There was a faint scorch mark where the photograph had been. When he'd completed the incantation to summon Hevring there had been the satisfactory flash of fire that he'd anticipated, but the picture had flipped into the air as if caught by a sudden gust.

Johannesson looked around. There, on the floor at his feet was the photo. He picked it up and almost cursed. The edges were blackened and charred, but the image of the shaggy man in the purple shirt was intact in the middle of the paper.

What the master of Svalgsay didn't notice was what *had* been burned away from the photo – a shadow on the wall behind John B. Eidur Johannesson's own shadow.

Still clutching the damaged picture, the man in black strode over to his obsidian bowl. Ideally he should add more of his mystic salt, but there should be enough potency left for a spell to work briefly. Long enough to… yes, the waters were rippling. He could see… he could see… his own island? The Australian was starting to climb the jagged perimeter of Svalgsay?

Very well. That could be managed. Let the rocks of the Swallower be the last things this aggravating fellow ever saw.

Returning to the beautifully decorated table, Eidur once again placed the photograph at the centre. He knew just the right incantation, knew just what to summon. The unstoppable, implacable thing called the Boyg.

John B. was picking a cautious way up the steep rock face. It wasn't easy, or pleasant, but frankly he'd had worse. The nightmare climb up a cliff in Hawaii sprang to mind, although then the ghosts of some ancient warriors had helped him. But 'up' was certainly better than 'down', and there was plenty of light to see by.

And then there wasn't.

It was as if John B. had been suddenly struck totally blind. There were no vague outlines, not even degrees of darkness. Just total, absolute black. This went beyond a mere absence of light, this was a darkness that could be felt.

Abruptly the wizard realized that wasn't just a turn of phrase inside his head – it was 100% accurate. He could still feel the stone under his hands, and through the soles of his deck shoes. But on the bare skin of his arms, face and scalp there was something more. Damp like fog, but more substantial, as if there was wet cloth against his skin.

He'd stopped moving as soon as the light disappeared. There didn't seem much choice. But now as he clung to the cliff like a limpet he was becoming disoriented. The darkness seemed to move around him. Up and down were no longer as obvious as they should be, and on a piece of jagged rock above the ocean that was not a good thing to realise.

Now there was a sound, like rushing wind. In spite of himself, Stewart felt compelled to move – to let go of the rock and ride the wind, giving in to the blackness. Somewhere in the wind he felt, as much as heard, a voice. "The Great Boyg conquers, but does not fight…" said the voice, somewhere between a whisper and a rumble.

John B. clenched his fingers, and jammed his feet hard against the rock wall. Suddenly he knew what to do. With all the care he could muster, he slowly moved his left hand toward the pocket of his jeans. He was so disoriented he had to slide his fingertips along the side of his own body, or he may never have found the pocket.

Questing fingers found the hard-shelled case, and as delicately as a safe-cracker unfastened and opened the lid. Carefully he extracted the mobile phone and then clutched it tightly. There was no point in trying to look at it. He could have rested it on the tip of his nose and still not been able to see it.

He moved his thumb around the device. Damn, but he hated technology! Could he remember what to do, where to press, without sight to guide him? He thought back to Q's instructions. In his mind's eye he saw those beautiful long fingers working across the phone. Very, very slowly his left thumb duplicated those movements.

And then the little device erupted into music. Music and words. Vivian Stanshall's voice, dramatically announcing, "And introducing, tubular bells!"

The great chimes pealed out over the guitars and other instrumentation of Oldfield's masterpiece. The volume wasn't loud, but it didn't have to be. With a sibilant sigh, the black mass of the Boyg fell apart, shredding like wet tissue paper. The daylight returned.

Grinning, the wizard returned the phone to his pocket, but let the music play on as he resumed his climb. The track finished just as he reached the top of the cliff.

Eidur stared at his altar. The swirl of dense smoke had disappeared, and there the wretched picture still lay. Blackened a little by soot, maybe, but intact. What sort of magic was this man protected by?

He walked over to the obsidian bowl. The water was dark, its occult power spent. It would take time to restore its effectiveness, but then Eidur realised that there was no need. The Australian was on the island. Where else could he go but here, to the sanctum?

It took only a few moments for Johannesson to set his steel-and-leather chair facing the unlocked door. It took not many more moments for him to reach into one of his cupboards and draw out a sleek automatic pistol. He loaded the gun, then sat and waited for his visitor.

John B. was in no hurry. Clearly this wasn't a big place. What – *who* he sought shouldn't be too hard to find. A few minutes' walk later, he saw the dome. At first he thought it was a natural mound. The coarse grass stood out against the surrounding rock but the walls of the basin in which it sat would provide some protection from the wind and salt spray. It was the shape that gave it away – a little too perfect.

The wizard shrugged. There was no point in subterfuge. He walked around the dome until he found the door, and knocked.

"Enter, please. It is not locked."

"Sorry if I drip on your floor. I'm still a bit damp," Stewart said casually as he stepped inside and closed the door behind himself.

“I appreciate your concern, but it is of no consequence.”

“Mind if I sit down? It’s been a long day.” Stewart had seen the gun, but knew the man facing him played a long tactical game, not an impulsive one. He was banking on a certain amount of intrigue in his opponent’s mind. He was right.

 The hand not holding the gun indicated a kitchen chair. “Of course. Please, be seated. You survived at sea, and then after,” observed Eidur with controlled polite interest.

“The Boyg. Yeah. Call it luck, or call it magic, or call it sheer bloody determination to find the man responsible for the shooting of the woman I love. But here I am.”

“How did you even know…?”

“About the big shapeless black bugger? And its aversion to the sound of bells? I studied *Peer Gynt* in a high school drama class. Great piece of theatre, if a bit long. Henrik Ibsen’s work is appreciated outside of Scandinavia, you know. Funny coincidence, that you’d summon up a critter I know from that play, especially when you consider that back in the 1860’s Ibsen was vehemently anti-German. He reckoned Norway hadn’t done enough to support Denmark in her struggle with Germany. Ironic given your Nazi sympathies.”

“I am not a Nazi,” replied Johannesson without rancour.

“There’s a saying in Australia – look like a crow, sound like a crow, get shot like a crow.”

 Eidur sneered and replied, “You do not understand who and what I am.”

“I understand you’re a man with a lot of blood on your hands.”

“No! I have killed no one.”

"Point taken, I suppose. Up to a point," Stewart said with a mirthless grin. "You're no executioner, are you? You sign the death warrant but you don't carry out the sentence. You're an arranger. A manipulator."

"I am content to allow others to be the means to my ends. The German and the Englishman who for a time were useful. The ancients I summon and direct with the power of the Odinspear. They kill. I do not need to. I am a man with a mission. My mission is to restore balance. To this country, perhaps to the world."

"Balance?"

"Yes."

"Ah, right. Your sister explained your history to me, and what you'd set out to do."

"She and I, together we restore the balance of this nation. We are correcting the great mistake of the past and bringing back to the proper balance."

"Rather different approaches, the two of you," the wizard said casually.

The man in black seemed equally relaxed, confident in his sanctum. "Indeed. Again, it is balance. I the sacred, she the secular."

It suddenly occurred to him to wonder when the Australian had spoken to Inge. Where had they met? How had he known her, or had she recognised him?

If Stewart noticed his host's puzzlement he gave no sign of it, his tone still diffident as he said, "Meaning, you're above actually getting your hands dirty, whereas she didn't mind taking an active role in proceedings."

"Indeed. As you say…" Eidur paused, frowning. "Didn't…? What do you mean *didn't*?"

"You really don't know what you've done, do you? Oops, that's a shame," said Stewart with a total absence of sincerity.

"What are you talking about?"

"Do you know how I got to this island?"

"By boat, obviously. There is no other way."

"Do you know whose boat? I was on the *Svalgsay*. Your sister was bringing me here, to confer with you on how to dispose of me. I think she had the idea that rather than killing me casually, in her usual manner, because you'd expressed an interest in me the two of you should decide together what *modus operandi* would be appropriate. What a pity she didn't get the chance to bring you up to date. I take it you were responsible for the destruction of the *Svalgsay*, like you were for the death of Miskwa Burns."

Only a serious conscious effort prevented Eidur's jaw from hanging open. He slumped heavily in his chair.

"This cannot be."

"Oh yes it can. I was tied up in the fishing boat when whatever the hell it was happened. There were two of us on that vessel. Only one was killed. Clearly, it wasn't me. I washed ashore, managed to get past the Boyg as discussed, and made my way here."

Eidur remained in his chair, still reluctant, or perhaps unable, to accept Stewart's account of the fate of his sister. How could he not have known? He mumbled his disbelief.

"I can take you to see the wreckage if you like." There was no emotion in John B.'s voice.

"Wreckage?"

"Yeah. It's off a sharp little point over that-a-way. Half a dozen low sharp spikes of rock poking up out of the waves, and a cliff behind. The cliff where you sent the Boyg."

Eidur jumped up and ran from the dome, ignoring the Australian, oblivious even to the gun in his own hand.

John B. walked over to the table that was the centre of Eidur's occult power. First he retrieved the photograph of himself, pocketing it safely. Then for a few moments he examined the Odinspear and the ornate setting in which it rested. He sighed.

"I don't reckon you're a safe thing to leave lying around," he said quietly.

He picked up the ancient artifact, and turned it over in his hands. He considered trying to break it over his knee, but realised he'd be more likely to break his knee in the attempt. With a shrug he jammed the wood into a deep pocket of his jeans, and unhurriedly walked out of the dome, following in the Norwegian's footsteps.

The wizard was unaware of it, but he was moving in just the measured, methodical way that Eidur Johannesson typically did. Or had, up until the news about his sister. The surviving twin hadn't recognised it in himself, but Inge's death had caused a profound change. He was unbalanced.

The blonde man had broken into a run – something he scarcely ever did since childhood. Stewart followed implacably behind at a casual, even pace. It wasn't a big island. Even if he couldn't see the man he pursued, he had a good idea of where he was going.

Sure enough, there he was, right by the cliff that the wizard had managed to scale despite the attentions of the Boyg. He was staring down, over the edge.

"I'm not usually one to say, 'I told you so', but in this case…"

Hearing the Australian's voice behind him, Eidur turned, wide-eyed and wild-eyed.

He frantically whipped his head back and forth, alternately staring at his nemesis and the wreckage, and nearby that the floating corpse of the woman who had been, in a very real sense, his other half. He finally, fatally, lost his balance and pitched over the edge of the cliff, still clutching the gun he'd never used.

It wasn't a long fall. It could have been dived, or even jumped, fairly safely. That however would have required a certain amount of clear-headedness. Alas for Eidur he was in no state for any sort of rational thought. His plunge into the sea had landed him in one of the *Svalgsay*'s fishing nets. At another time he could have stayed calm, disentangled himself, and swum free. This was not that time.

The Norwegian flailed and thrashed, snaring himself further in the strands.

From above, John B. watched as the maddened man in the water inadvertently cracked himself in the head with a fragment of broken decking. It was a glancing blow, ordinarily harmless. But it was enough to momentarily stun, and provoke a sharp automatic intake of breath – unfortunate for a man whose mouth and nose were underwater. Caught in the net, his lungs filled quickly.

As his struggles ceased, the action of the waves succeeded in bobbing him free of the worst of the net's snare. Stewart stood for a while longer, watching the two bodies drawn together by the sea. Inge face up, her brother face down – side by side for a moment they resembled a *yin* and *yang* symbol. Their own balance seemed to be restored in death.

With neither a word nor a gesture John B. turned and walked away. With unhurried steps he started to trace the perimeter of Svalgsay island. It didn't take long for him to find what he knew must be there somewhere – the small jetty and Johannesson's launch.

He had enough nautical knowledge to start the motor and head for Bergen. As he travelled, he mused. Would the two bodies make it to the shore of the mainland, found and declared a tragic mystery? Pieces of the wreckage of the *Svalgsay* would eventually wash ashore and be found. There might be some who would wonder at the captain setting out on her own without a crew, or perhaps not. Maybe she did that often, visiting her brother on his island.

What about the island? Was there someone to claim possession of it, and all it contained? Eidur's 'mentor' perhaps. As far as Stewart was concerned the whole bloody place could crumble to dust and blow into the ocean.

He made one stop on the journey.

Off his port bow was a place where a great glacier reached the open sea. He pulled the boat in beside the ice wall and stopped the motor. As the boat bobbed, the wizard detached the launch's anchor from its chain. It required a satisfying amount of effort to wedge the Odinspear into the iron eye of the anchor. A length of polypropylene rope was wrapped in such a way as to give some added security to the 'join'.

With great care and no ceremony John B. dropped the object overboard, to sink into the dark depths. He didn't care how many years – decades, centuries, or millennia it would take for the glacier to roll over the weighted relic. He was the only person who knew it was there, and he wouldn't be telling anyone.

Even if the mystical wood survived its immersion it would never be found by an aspiring Adolf Hitler or Eidur Johannesson, anyone who might attempt to control a power that was, in truth, beyond human capacity to control.

He set off again for Bergen. He was exhausted, but knew he would have the energy to get to the Lemon and drive up to the farm. There would be a story to tell the Mapletons – the adults at least, but most of that could wait until tomorrow. All he wanted was to fall into the arms of his green eyed pretty lady, his own *fior ghaol*.

.oOo.

26 CLEARING THE BOARD

John B. and his beloved stayed on the farm for another couple of weeks while Elizabeth regained her strength. Stewart did some fencing, both kinds, and pitched in with other jobs. They even both returned to the chess club to be warmly welcomed. Kevin Bischoff wasn't there. Neither he nor Eidur Johannesson had been seen recently, they were told.

The Australians took a quiet decision not to enlighten the police on Shetland, about what they knew or suspected about Inge's crimes or the death of Miskwa Burns. Where could they even begin an explanation?

"It'll remain a cold case that will only get colder," said John B. with a shrug.

A parcel arrived at the farm for John B. It contained a dapper waistcoat made from the purple tartan cloth and an exquisitely matched purple satin. The remaining tartan had been used to make a striking pair of trousers.

They tried to contact Hannah to say thanks, and arrange payment. Her assistant Astrid explained that the boss had suddenly left town 'on business', but had advised that no invoice was to be prepared. The clothes were a gift, apparently.

What was most intriguing was that the vest and trousers fitted perfectly, despite no measurements having ever been taken. Hannah hadn't seen John B. again since the day of Q's shooting, when Anna had given the cloth to the seamstress just after she arrived.

"How did she get the size so exactly right?" Elizabeth asked Anna over dinner the night the parcel arrived.

"She's got a good eye, I'd say," suggested John B. He wished he'd had a lot more time to talk with the woman called the Weaver.

As welcome as they were made to feel by all of the Mapleton clan, the Australian couple decided it was time to take their leave. Elizabeth had been writing copiously, transcribing her notes and story onto a new 'tablet' that John B. had bought for her in Bergen.

The aspiring author felt she'd done all that she could with her Shetland and Norwegian research. Now she wanted to explore the 'discovery of America' connection – perhaps even try to retrace the footsteps of 'Prince Henry' St. Clair.

John B. had no objection to travelling to the US, but did make one request.

"Let's not sail over, hey? I think I've had enough for a while. The *True Love* can stay here on indefinite loan to Edmund if he wants it. Or we can sell her. But this trip, I really would rather fly, pretty lady."

"That's fine with me, babe. I think that's fair. Leave it to me to arrange."

"Why ma'am, ah wouldn't have it any other way," John B. drawled with a grin.

On their last night in Bergen the whole family went for a night out at a picturesque hotel up on the mountainside overlooking the city. The day's faint fall of snow still lay on tree branches and windowsills, catching the twinkle of the lights below. It was a scene from a postcard, and the food and drink were just as perfect.

Over dinner Q presented John B. with the pendant she'd bought in Hannah's store.

"Something to remember Norway by," she said, laughing.

"As if I'd ever forget this place," Stewart laughed in reply as she fixed the leather cord around his neck and told its story.

"Oh my!" she said suddenly. "I just realised, it must have been in my pocket when I was shot!"

John B. hugged his beloved and said, "It's beautiful, darling, and believe me, I *will* treasure it. All the more so for knowing the old Viking protection worked for you."

Chortling, Edmund suggested, "The Vikings are long gone, you'd think their magic must have disappeared."

With a serious frown on her small face Ivy chided him. "Daddy, magic doesn't disappear. You just have to know where to look for it."

Ed laughed, not unkindly, but amused at being put in his place by his little daughter. Anna laughed too, though not before wondering for just a moment what ideas their two guests might have put in their children's heads.

Having the 'kidlets' with them meant it wasn't a late night, but at this time of year the sky was dark early. Up here, well away from the lights of the port city, the stars shone like a spray of diamonds on a black cloth. Over their final round of hot chocolate (with or without a dash of something stronger) all six of them were gazing out the restaurant window.

Suddenly there was movement in the sky. Moving light, like strips of a delicate fabric drifting in the air.

"The aurora borealis! Oh JB, that's the first time I've seen the Northern Lights!" exclaimed Elizabeth.

"Up here we call them the Merry Dancers," said Little Don, a moment before his father could say exactly the same thing.

"I can see why," agreed the brunette. "They're beautiful."

Both adult couples held hands as they gazed out on the spectacular display. It was as if Norway was putting on a special farewell show, just for Q and John B. – a fitting end to a fine night.

The next morning Edmund did the 'delivery run' to the airport. He couldn't stay, there was work to be done on the farm, where the rest of his family waited, still a little teary from embraces and fond farewells. The affection was mutual. John B., not normally fond of children, had become close to his old friend's offspring, and Elizabeth had come to care deeply for the whole family. They had looked after her when she needed them most, and they'd all won a place in her heart.After a final lingering embrace – for Elizabeth like being hugged by two adoring bears – the farmer gave one last wave and drove off in the Lemon.

The departure formalities went smoothly. Bergen airport was much less hectic than the last time John B. had been in the terminal. With some time before their flight was due to leave, the couple settled in the comfortable café.

Q sat at a small table, waiting for her beau to return from the bar. A distinguished figure in a pale grey suit and dark glasses stopped beside her, and bowed. It was Kevin Bischoff.

"Excuse me – aren't you the young lady who was staying with the Mapletons?" he asked politely.

Elizabeth nodded, momentarily puzzled. Bischoff introduced himself, explaining that they'd met briefly at the chess club. He enquired after her health, expressing his sincere regret at the 'unfortunate incident' that he'd heard had befallen her.

Vaguely recognising the man now, the brunette thanked him for his concern and invited him to join them for a drink.

"Alas, I must decline – I have already heard the final call for my flight. I am on my way to Rome on business. A great pity, as I would very much like to talk with you. Next time."

As he turned to walk away he realised that John B. Stewart was standing behind him, saying nothing but staring grimly.

The grey-suited man leaned close to the Australian and in a low voice growled, "My race is older even than yours, magic user. We are even more patient, as well as more powerful. I wonder if, perhaps, the time for patience is gone, and it is time for us to assert that power. We will meet again, son of the islands."

He shook himself slightly, as if settling ruffled feathers, and strode to his departure gate.

John B. put the glasses down on the table. The magic still buzzed at the back of his brain as it seemed to always do, but now there was a definite warning tone to it.

"What was that all about?" asked Q, who hadn't been able to catch much of the parting remark.

"I honestly have no idea."

"Don't stress about it, babe. If it's important I'm sure we'll see him again somewhere. Never mind. Here's cheers – to old family ties."

That provoked a puzzled expression from the wizard, even as he raised his glass in response.

"Prince Henry, and the old American settlement we're going looking for," she explained.

John B. smiled in response, and clinked his tumbler of single malt against the proffered glass of chardonnay. It was breakfast time in Norway, but somewhere in the world the sun was over the yardarm, and the world was theirs to explore.

He replied, "To family ties, old friends, and new horizons." He looked into the eyes of the woman he'd come so close to losing and added, "And to being with the one I love."

That was a toast they both thought worth drinking to.

- ENDE -

The *Dubious Magic* Books:

THE WIZARD OF WARAMANGA

THE CARVINGS OF COBBEMARMOO

THE MAD MACHINES OF MUNDARA

THE WARRIORS OF WIWO'OLE

THE SPIRITS OF SRON DUBH

Visit **www.renoirwords.com**
or
www.patreon.com/Renoir

Next: Twenty-first Century Maine still has a lot of old world charm. But
there are some echoes of the past that are anything but benign.
Monsters on land and sea, and a band of unlikely but ruthless pirates.
On a search for family history, John B. and Elizabeth find much more than
they'd bargained for - perhaps more than even the wizard's strange power
can contend with.

THE TREASURE OF TEPATAMWA
The Seventh Book of Dubious Magic

9 780994 617569